T0129439

Orgasmic Catalog

Written and Illustrated by

Wendy McNally

Order this book online at www.trafford.com
or email orders@trafford.com

Most Trafford titles are also available at major online book retailers.

Print information available on the last page.

This is a work of fiction. All the characters and events portrayed in this book are
fictitious, and any resemblance to real people or events is purely coincidental.

ISBN: 978-1-4120-2368-9 (sc)
ISBN: 978-1-4122-2213-6 (e)

Because of the dynamic nature of the Internet, any web addresses or links contained in
this book may have changed since publication and may no longer be valid. The views
expressed in this work are solely those of the author and do not necessarily reflect the
views of the publisher, and the publisher hereby disclaims any responsibility for them.

Any people depicted in stock imagery provided by Thinkstock are models,
and such images are being used for illustrative purposes only.
Certain stock imagery © Thinkstock.

Trafford rev. 11/03/2016

www.trafford.com

North America & international
toll-free: 1 888 232 4444 (USA & Canada)
fax: 812 355 4082

Table of Contents:

Excerpts From Helena's Book: "The Three Sisters"

4

List of Poems:

List of Recipes:

Chapter 1
Laying The Egg Before Poaching It

As the first and last born of parents dedicated to tilling and prospering from the land, the young prepubescent Helena fantasized a life of storytelling and adventures with imagined siblings, playmates and gypsies.

By birth, she entered into a Kingdom where porridge grains cooked with raisins and cane sugar, constituted the daily breakfasts that sustained her throughout her early years. Weekly school lunches of thinly sliced beef tongue and chicken liver pate' graced the space between thick slices of fresh baked bread.

At the end of each studious day, a bus ride home rewarded Helena with an abundance of other common local fare and main courses designed to nourish discriminating palates sanctioned by unknown delicacy-obsessed immigrant forefathers.

Oven roasted pork heart with asparagus, liver with onions, pan-fried tripe and kidney with mushrooms, boiled chicken feet and giblets in seasoned broth, pickled vegetables, and jellied meats were among several of the savory evening dinner servings available in her mother's kitchen.

However, with the advent of puberty, Helena fervently drew inspiration from the verifiable practicality of her realistic, pastoral environment. Between school sessions, she no longer desired her previously contrived semblance of fantasized companionships and social idealism.

Helena's solitariness represented a new and significant challenge, one that invited independence, exploration and growth. To quell her rising pubertal instincts, the vulnerable fertile adolescent felt herself becoming a culinary Goddess: smelling, tasting and touching everything encyclopedically edible.

Flat-chested in appearance and boyish in her demeanor, fourteen year old Helena was determined to become a woman. After all, she was a girl;

although, having periods made her feel more like a wounded animal than a sexual or reproductive beauty when compared to other girls her own age with bolstered buttocks and voluptuous bosoms that poured out of their school uniforms like over risen bread dough.

As much as Helena loved to climb trees and make elaborate weapons out of rubber bands and sticks for the purpose of targeting small animals from her lofty tree branch in her backyard, it seemed no longer an appropriate pastime for a diametrically maturing young Diva. Instead, she gathered eggs from the henhouse to use in her experimental food preparations.

Being as naïve to the kitchen as any boy might be, Helena's cooking began with great excitement, caution and trepidation. Her first courageous act was the simple culinary practice of poaching an egg. Enhanced with salt, pepper, butter, grated cheese, chopped green onions, garden herbs and a drizzle of fresh cream, Helena had replaced the timeless bowls of porridge. The daily enchantment she experienced during breakfast was enough to stir within her pubescent interior, a self-indulgent desire for sexual pleasure that she felt compelled to study in her bedroom mirror.

Standing naked and spindly as a willow tree in winter, she touched her infinitesimally small erupting breasts and stroked her private, diabolically divine pubic bud, as gently as she petted newborn kittens and featherless baby birds. In an undecipherable passage of time, Helena surrendered to a fascinating overture of wavelike tidal sensations that careened throughout her entire body. The ebb and flow of soothing rhythms, the rise and fall of unmastered contractions that gripped her torso and extremities, tumbled her into a state of dream-like powerlessness.

Eclipse after eclipse, she climaxed with her own unrelenting, undulating mirrored reflection while gloriously digesting her morning feast of dairy delights. Helena was temporarily spellbound and exhausted. Her altered state of compositional awareness rendered her captive to a previously unknown phenomenon of orgasmic magnitude. She fell to her knees, then repositioned her willowy limbs inside her clothes.

Henceforth, gathering eggs became a ritual of pious proportions. The frequency and familiarity of the egg collecting episodes finally led one day, to the unavoidable question with respect to evolutionary order. The dilemma occurred on a particularly early morning at sunrise when Helena, upon entering the henhouse, startled a hen in the second quarter of her deliverance.

The winged creature jolted upright as if to take flight. However, the alarmed bird was forced to abort the aerial mission due to the precarious state of her egg. It had fiercely seized at its pinnacle of indecisiveness by the constriction of its reproductive pathway. The semi-protruding object, unable to retreat or eject, remained in stasis giving the hen an undeniable expression of electrifying orgasmic precision.

Helena embarrassingly recognized the manifestation. It appeared identical to the vivid shock of suspended revelry during her erotic self-gratification in front of the looking glass.

Confused and distraught, Helena left the henhouse that morning without gathering any eggs. The unexpected interruption of an otherwise normal sequence of events disturbed her focus and caused her to deeply contemplate the origin and structure of the universe. Was it chaotic or was it organized? Was it dispersed or was it compressed? Which really came first, the chicken or the egg?

Helena mentally tabulated and arranged her thoughts over a comforting bowl of porridge and did not touch herself for days.

Poem #1
When We Were Children

Each year,
We became the wheat.
We grew,
Then we were harvested.

Mother's sunburned breasts,
Swayed
With the swaying gold bristles
Of the wheat

As she walked with the farmers
To the swather and combine
Every day,
Until the snow came.

Then in her winter dress
And autumn scarf
Tied around her head,
She primed a batch of dough.

With thick palms pressing down,
Pressing down,
Round and round,
She turned us into bread.

Recipe #1
Philosopher's Omelet For One

-Heat a skillet with a moderate measure of olive oil.
-Add scissor snipped pieces of mildly spiced raw Italian pork sausage, chopped green onions, crushed garlic, sliced mushrooms, and young beet leaves.
-Simmer and toss gently.
-Flavor with very small amounts of sweet sherry, white wine and Teriyaki sauce.
-Sprinkle heavily with dry Romano cheese and grated Mozzarella cheese.
-Add as many slightly beaten raw eggs (2-4) as needed to completely surround the simmered ingredients.
-Season with a sprinkle of sea salt and chopped sprigs of fresh dill.
-Stir the eggs in and around the ingredients to combine evenly.
-Place a double layer of sliced Provolone cheese on top of the entire surface.
-Lift the omelet in segments, repeatedly while rotating the pan, permitting the eggs to set and the liquids to concentrate.
-Cover and allow the omelet to simmer undisturbed, until the cheese is fully melted, the eggs appear cooked and the liquids are reduced.
-Loosen the omelet from the pan, and then fold it in half upon itself.
-Slide the countryside meal onto a single pre-warmed oval plate in the shape a fleeing rabbit.

Presentation:
-Serve yourself outdoors, early on a cool morning.
-Eat alone, curled up under a tree beside a riverbank, and quietly evaluate orbital courses, cosmic forces and terrestrial resources.
-End your solitary meal with a deep breath and a daydream of a perfect mate with whom to share the contents of your meditative plate.

Recipe #2
Philosopher's Omelet For Several

-Heat a skillet with a generous measure of olive oil.
-Add raw baby scallops, shrimp, thin wedges of Spanish onions, sliced mushrooms, young spinach leaves and a few leaves of basil.
-Simmer and toss gently.
-Flavor with moderate amounts of sweet sherry, white wine and oyster sauce.
-Sprinkle heavily with dry Parmesan cheese and grated Asiago cheese.
-Add as many slightly beaten raw eggs (6-10) as needed to completely surround simmered ingredients.
-Season with a grating of fresh black pepper, a light sprinkle of mild red chili peppers, sea salt and chopped sprigs of fresh thyme.
-Stir eggs in and around all of the ingredients to combine evenly.
-Simmer covered and undisturbed, until the contents are fused.
-Loosen the omelet and slide onto a circular oiled blue ceramic dish carved in the shape of a fish.
-Place a thick layer of sliced Mozzarella and Edam cheeses on the surface of the omelet.
-Cover the cheeses with a final garnish of sliced tomatoes, a generous scatter of sliced black olives and crumbled Feta cheese.
-Place the entire open round of omelet uncovered in an oven at 350 degrees, until the contents are sizzling and the cheeses are melted.
-Serve slightly cooled.
-Share this meal of casual complicatedness with eccentric, witty, unselfish and supportive friends of extraordinary delightfulness.
-Provide a side dish of toasted fruit bread with honey and cream cheese.

Presentation:
-Serve to invited friends, outside on a warm patio deck at noon.
-Allow a white vinyl material to cover a large picnic table.
-Add corner weights of contentious sun-dried cow skulls, previously acquired by means of bartered goods.
-Announce the presence of iridescent blue and green peacock feathers held captive in a cobalt blue vase.

-The feathers will shimmer from a light breeze and from heavy laughter.
-A harmonious blend of teas and lightly spirited fruit juices may inspire visionary answers to a stream of revolutionary quandaries.
-If the meal ends and you are still without a mate, wait.
-Your mental state can flirt with fate, but love is in the weather with an unpretentious date.

Chapter 2
No Turning Back Now...Once A Cook Always A Cook

Helena labored over the kitchen stove concentrating on devising lunch. Breakfast preparations had already subsided when Helena's sleeping schedule fell toward noon.

She cooked only on weekends and only for herself. It wasn't a narcissistic exploitation; it was simply the arrangement her parents preferred. Being an only child and intellectually agile student, Helena was excused from most onerous non-scholastic duties at her country home. Weekdays were academic sojourns for Helena and weekends became lustful preoccupations with remedies to satisfy her physical and psychological hungers.

At the gallant age of sixteen, Helena's sexual awareness and curiosity had reached a forbidden height as did her desires to nurture fantasies conceptualizing the as yet, elusive, intangible male.

Helena's anticipation for love and sex resulted in an intense flourish of poetic verse and tantalizing recipes. As she summoned the wisdom of ancient deities and dynasties, a tureen of luscious coriander, cumin and fenugreek stew emerged steaming hot from Helena's oven.

Her midday creation, laden with spiced sausages, carrots, peas, leeks and potatoes incensed the air with tempting aromas. Helena consecrated the stew with a splash of yogurt and a light grating of nutmeg, then escorted her sumptuous meal to the barnyard where the horses languished in the warm spring sun.

The black stallion was already displaying his fully charged, graciously enlarged equine alter piece while emitting gentle deep throated rumbling sounds to a chorus of song birds circling overhead. A quivering mare stood waiting nearby.

Clad in her jeans and hand knit jacket, Helena descended comfortably onto a throne of thick soft grass against the barn wall. The heavily scented stew tasted more delicious than she ever imagined. Spoonful after spoonful, the flavor was sinfully arresting.

Equally, the stallion's ensuing theatrical copulation with his incumbent mate was sinfully arousing. As Helena visually absorbed the captivating rapture between stud and mare, she unexpectedly lost her composure as an uncontrollable orgasm spontaneously erupted within her inner sanctum.

She firmly grasped her bowl of remaining stew and waited for her quake and aftershocks to settle. Did Goddesses often come this way, she wondered apprehensively? Did the laws of nature and cosmic structure permit such random flexibility and insurrection?

Exhausted and intrigued, Helena decided that this erotic indecency was definitely for the priest. She didn't believe in a God, but confessing her sins while still under her parents' guardianship was a necessary and ponderously uninspiring exercise. It was an expectation she felt obliged to fulfill.

The following day, Helena entered the school chapel at the end of the daily morning mass. Step by step, through a nauseating heavy odor of lingering incense, she was destined for the confessional. Considering the private holy sanctuaries confessionals represented, the affairs and secrets that whispered through the course weave of the window which divided the sinner from the confessor, followed by the questions, absolution and penance that whispered back, were at times, blasphemous.

When Helena confessed her bestial induced immorality, the priest menacingly turned toward the coarsely woven window and demanded to know her full name. Helena could smell the clergyman's wicked breath, scented by the stale body and blood of the holy sacrament of communion, the cannibalistic liturgical excuse for non-punishable habitual over-consumption and evil conduct.

Helena panicked; then she lied. In a steady unflinching voice, she uttered the first and last name of a female classmate, one whom Helena thought deserved an anonymous clobbering for stealing her diary notes and passing them around the class in shrouded secrecy and jest.

The priest, unable to decipher the truth of a sinner's admissions, issued Helena a stern ecclesiastical warning and prayers from the entire rosary, bead by bead, on her knees. He also insisted that she join him in private prayer that evening in his holy sacristy.

Helena, however, was already aware of the priest's temple of unchaste perverse acts of contrition. She over heard rumors and testimonials in dimly lit school stairwells and dark corners of hallways, detailing the priest's various methods of reconnaissance for the purpose of redeeming the Almighty's fallen flock. Absolution by physical and sexual punishment was the clergyman's preferred modus operandi, ensconcing nearly the entire parish of devout, God-fearing men, women and children.

With the stinging wrath of the Lord upon her; Helena like a stray lamb, left the house of God in utter defiance. She completely ignored the hallowed penance and questionable invitation to further repent in the private sanctity of the priest's dungeon and instead, went jogging. Casual sprinting was an activity that allowed her to disregard reality while conjuring up recipes and poetry, as if they belonged to each other.

Poem #2
Beaver Dam

A silent pond spread like a net:

Triangular,
Starless,
Complete.

The depth held the natives
Unseen;

The willowy trees were wet
To their bellies;

And that certain single smell of green
Kept disappearing.

The dam controlled the collective
While the natives
Struggled to survive.

The rhythmic dipping of my paddle
Celebrated a cosmic bond.

The hidden traps of the hunter
Assaulted a sacred pond.

My gratitude came by day;
The hunter came
By night.

My solitude bereaved the dead;
The hunter intruded,
Then fled.

Poem #3
Dead Beaver

I touched a heavy sleeping mound
As if expecting something warm, as if

Uncertain of a sudden breath or bound.
But its stillness was too anchored;

Its coldness was too sound.
The bloodless corpse had tiny ears

With velvet on the insides;
And at the very tender tips

Where only thunder could hide,
Frozen raindrops fit.

The smooth curled flesh felt like
edges of rose petals.

The trapper thought he fooled me

Into thinking I had come upon

A wild untamed creature
Sullened by my gentle arm.

Recipe #3
Luscious Lobster Lunch For Lazy Summer Days

-Simmer in salted cream, white wine, crushed garlic and butter: small lobster tails, clusters of baby bok choy and whole young mushrooms.
-Add chopped dill weed and chopped green onions, along with a handful of precooked pasta.
-Serve hot with fresh bread sticks, sesame crackers and caraway seed buns.
-Prepare your favorite salad greens and garden vegetables with thick yogurt lemon dressing to dip.
-Follow with chilled pre-cooked shrimp dredged in sweet, spicy apricot/mango/mustard sauce.
-Finish with puff pastry shells, filled with raspberries, a drizzle of pear liqueur and generous mounds of whipped cream.

Presentation:
-Serve outdoors on an umbrella shaded bedroom patio.
-Cover an outdoor table with a woven straw mat graciously adorned with seashells, rugged pieces of driftwood and stones worn smooth from ocean tides.
-Accent the table with a tall brass box heralding dune grass.
-If you are offered compliments and kisses during the meal, accept them affably.

Recipe #4
Samba Salad

-Combine cooled pre-cooked petite pasta with pre-cooked, chilled shrimp and crabmeat.
-Add sliced black olives, chilled sliced mushrooms pre-fried in garlic, olive oil and port wine.
-Add chopped raw green onions and slivered roasted red peppers.
-Toss with assorted greens: lettuce, spinach and watercress.
-Dress with a creamy sweet orange juice and mint vinaigrette.
-Add a liberal grating of fresh Parmesan and Asiago cheese.
-Combine with a gentle toss.
-Before serving, arrange the top with sliced boiled eggs, crispy bacon, mango slices, avocado wedges, crumbled Feta cheese, fresh chopped tops of Italian parsley and peppergrass.
-Sprinkle with coarsely ground pepper and toasted garlic croutons.

Presentation:
-Serve indoors beside an open breezy window.
-Stir the visual palate with a black tablecloth and a large white vase of pink verbena.
-An invitation to stroll the beach with a blanket and a comprehensive seductive intent may follow.

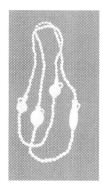

Chapter 3
Soufflé With A Kiss And A Warm Bath

Helena was nearly finished high school when she realized that her exterior being was finally extolling some notable feminine virtues. She hoped that soon she might be appreciated by more interesting human specimens than just the giddy, insecure female classmates whose identity crisis made them want to constantly touch her skin or stroke her curves, accidentally and intentionally.

The vibrant femme fatale was a powerful target for the lesbian fascination that dominated the girls' school she attended. But for Helena, girls did not arouse in her any emotions other than fight or flight. Girls functioned as boring companions and dull conversationalists at the best of times, and hostile jealous creatures the rest of the time.

Girls were semi-functional, uninspiring clones. They were replications, not unlike her father's herd of bovine conformities. Touching their teats would have been less than scintillating. Girl's kisses were dry and deceptive; their fondling was awkwardly cumbersome and loveless. Helena's conclusions were the result of embarrassing attempts against her purist heterosexual constitution during an unavoidable clandestine sleepover in the girl's dormitory after a late night study session in the library.

Having lost track of time, the tired susceptible Diva found herself enticed into a half night's sleep in the retirement quarters of her resident classmates. Upon their intrusive, nonconsensual violation of her private parts, Helena made a frantic exit from the objectionable predatory cast of scandalmongers. She scurried through dark wide hallways, ran clear of Private Teachers' Lounges and Student Cafeterias, descended granite stairways and eventually entered the Janitor's room where she curled up on an empty cot. The displaced, sleep deprived, emotionally wounded runaway rested for a few nightmarish hours until a stream of sunlight struck her face and awakened her before the in house staff and students began to stir.

Later, in the Phys-Ed shower room where all the girls were temporarily naked attended by their gymnasium supervisor and member of the sisterhood, the juvenile neophytes were visually scanned by the burly nun from inside her defensive cloak and habit. Helena, feeling extraordinarily secure and boldly superior, exposed her athletic but modestly developed physique with obvious pride and flamboyance. Her delicate musculature moved with assurance, ease and confidence as she undressed, cleansed herself and dressed again. Her dejected ambient classmates however, cowered shyly behind their surreptitious desires, blushed cheeks, unfulfilled sexual strategies and oversized towels.

Helena was solemnly preparing her mind and body for an exquisitely stimulating male companion, someone who would be an exalting lover and quintessential friend. The young Goddess's patience and integrity withstood the passing of final exams including her driver's license, a long awaited acquisition which bestowed upon her a most vital degree of freedom.

Without any impending foresight or intuitive sensibility, she finally met her elusive male one evening at the lake near her school. Helena was resting on the sandy beach watching the sun disappear when suddenly he was quietly sitting beside her. They both had been jogging around the body of water at spaced intervals.

Unknown to Helena, as she thoughtfully carved her poems and recipes, with each rhythmic step he had been behind her, training for the sports team at the boys' high school across the street from the convent. Sitting side by side, they talked and laughed with mounting acquaintance and trust. Nonchalantly, they slipped off their clothes and entered the lagoon.

The motionless water was soothing as a warm bath. As they relaxed near each other casually floating in circles, hours passed. They shared stories under moonlight, tiredly whispered goodbye and agreed to meet again the next evening.

Helena was demonstratively excited. The next day was Saturday, a cooking day and she had already been fearlessly skinny-dipping with someone named Napoleon. Should she give him a poem or just something candidly appetizing?

Naturally, she planned to share her extraordinary culinary talent with her newly discovered mate; her poetry she thought could wait. Helena occupied her kitchen all Saturday afternoon displaying great fervor and radiance as she prepared a ravishing dessert. It didn't take Helena long to decide that her Napoleon might appreciate the extravagance of a chocolate soufflé.

Perfectly baked and draped in streams of chocolate and flavored with spirits of rum, Helena guardedly delivered the gift that evening to her Napoleon by the lake. When she arrived, he was already there waiting for her, with a gift as well. For Helena, Napoleon held an iridescent white seashell with a blue topaz necklace nestled inside.

They sat down on the sand close to each other, cradling the warm bowl of soufflé and cupping the jewels between them. With each spoonful of dessert, Napoleon leaned toward Helena; with sensual grace, he embedded his damp lips on her forehead, on each cheek, then intently, on her lips.

Helena swayed with intoxication as the earth rocked under her. A surge of trembles flowed throughout her being and overtook her sense of judgment and rationale. Like a flock of internal migrating butterflies dislodging her center of gravity, she felt limp and disembodied. Helena was as dreamily captivated by every kiss, as Napoleon appeared genuinely captivated by each mouthful of soufflé until the bowl was empty.

Helena grew mildly perplexed as her Napoleon seductively smiled, then began to lick the inside of the bowl for any final remnants of ephemeral pleasure. He groaned and rhapsodized with each unctuous swirl of his tongue around the dish, until the feast was truly over. Napoleon's oral endeavor seemed comically onanistic, yet unobtrusive.

The evening continued in deliberate anticipated silence. Both Helena and Napoleon impulsively discarded their clothes and hesitated momentarily before entering the lake. Napoleon secured the string of faceted stones around Helena's neck as she shamelessly gazed at the strident Athenian attending to her. His juvenile regard for the soufflé was a display completely antithetical to his physical maturity. His muscular wealth and gracefully hung necessities reminded Helena of the quantifiably beautiful stallion in her yard. Without a moment of hesitation or mistrust, Helena stretched outward onto her back, suspended by the warm bath and her inner thoughts.

She began to seriously ponder the significance of the young man nibbling at her wet toes like minnows, when she pleasantly stirred to the meaning of a very special kiss, one that found its way up the watery pathway between her legs as she continued to lay suspended upon the lake. Napoleon's watery lips and tongue journeyed along her inner thighs to the entrance of her private orgasmic temple, then kissed and gently suckled her vulnerable bud of sensory sublimation. How did he know it was there? And how did he know of her longing to be seduced into such ecstasy? His capacity and appetite for indulgence was becoming obviously sacrosanct. Napoleon's slippery wet hands slowly caressed Helena's torso as they ascended towards her small plump pubescent breasts.

The erotic experience was enveloping Helena in a positively tranquil mission to the stars and back. She would certainly have to analyze the meaning of the epiphany later. The bowl licking sequence earlier seemed of little worrisome consequence now and perhaps it was even a necessary prelude to the ultimately angelic kiss between her thighs.

What if she had given Napoleon a poem? Would the planets have shifted out of their orbits? Would a coronation so triumphant have occurred in serious detriment of her youthful virginity for the dignity of a greater sphere of Wisdom, Fertility and Divinity?

Helena disengaged from her virtuous position on the water. As she stood on the sandy bottom of the lagoon, somewhat unsteadily, she drew Napoleon close to her. The warm bath water surrounded them as the air above cooled and the sky darkened. The topaz adornment glistened against Helena's wet skin.

With her arms wrapped around his sculpted torso, Helena graciously kissed Napoleon's lips. He thanked her for the chocolate soufflé, and Helena thanked him for making her feel like one. The evening ended with the young Goddess feeling uncertain of everything, including their next already planned encounter.

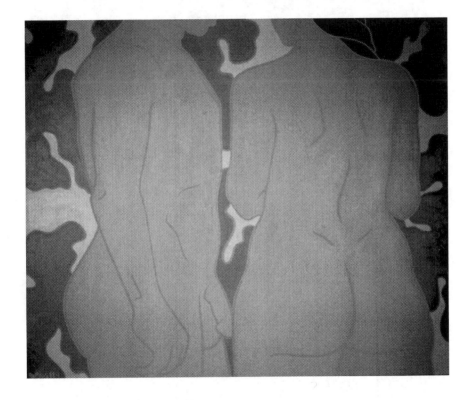

Poem #4
Island Guest

He clutched two knotted canes
As he shuffled along the path.

Pebbles rattled and sprayed
Around his small wobbling feet.

His head of powdery white hair
Wavered like the pink raspberries

That now and again
Tapped his cheek.

Age accosted the child
Quickly as youth fled.

He was a mother's babe still
And a rhyme from an old mill.

When his thin quaking voice emerged
Sounding like a crackling shell,

Then suddenly a bird, I had his eyes,
Faded as the evening sky.

Deep inside them vaguely shone,
A multitude of falling stars.

He was a tender sapling
Sucking hard at Nature's breast,

An ancient willow
Shaking from the weather.

Recipe #5
Lunch With A Bunch Of Bonnets

-Lightly toast fresh bread with a brushing of olive oil, balsamic vinegar and crushed garlic.
-Layer with thick slices of Brie cheese and fresh avocado.
-Salt and pepper the avocado.
-Drizzle with a creamy lemon dressing.
-Top with Teriyaki and honey marinated pre-grilled chicken breast.
-Place the open sandwich in an oven just long enough to warm through and slightly melt the cheese.
-On a side plate, serve with cottage cheese, whole olives and crescents of sweet apples.
-Adorn the side plate with red nasturtium flowers.

Presentation:
-Debate the pros and cons of country life over a checkered blue and white tablecloth enhanced with a vase of blue and white garden bonnets.
-A surprise serving of fresh blueberries, orange zest, maple syrup and whipped cream might temporarily resolve any disputes.

Recipe #6
Lunch With A Spray of Trumpets

-Lightly toast fresh bread with a brushing of olive oil, balsamic vinegar and crushed garlic.
-Layer with thick slices of Emmenthal cheese, mayonnaise, pre-grilled sliced artichoke hearts, a drizzle of lemon juice and sweet, hot mustard.
-Add shavings of smoked pastrami.
-Place the open sandwich in an oven just long enough to warm through and slightly melt the cheese.
-On a side plate, serve with raw carrots, cucumbers and celery.
-Garnish the vegetables with yellow nasturtium flowers.

Presentation:
-Debate the pros and cons of city life over a pale green tablecloth enhanced with a vase of pink garden trumpets.
-A surprise serving of fresh strawberries, sliced bananas, maple syrup and whipped cream should definitely suspend any differences of opinion.

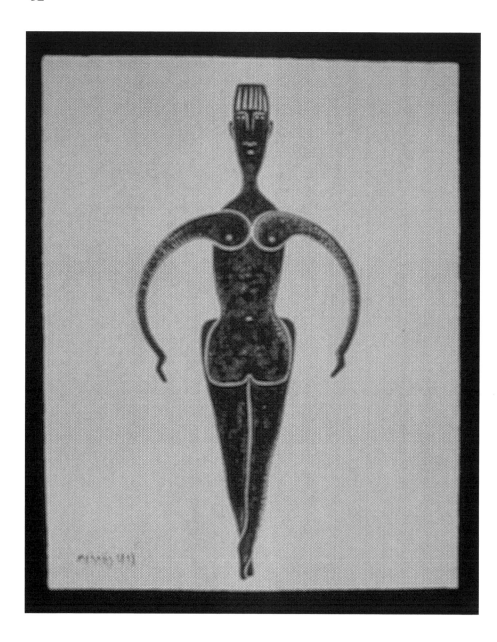

Chapter 4
Examining The Garden Naked

Weeks passed. The last tentatively scheduled engagement beside the lake did not occur. Helena stealthily avoided jogging to keep from accidentally encountering her magnificent male.

Occasionally, she saw him at a distance, but they only timidly waved to each other. Helena wasn't sure if their shy gestures of acknowledgement were drenched in longing for, or apprehension of each other.

Her recent recognition and acquisition of virginal rapture made her feel desperately in need of an emotional and physical hiatus; a retreat from the intensive exhilaration born of enlightenment; a charming excuse equivalent to nuns escaping the high school convent for similar respite in the Garden of Eden at a secluded rest home, far away from students and daily sacrifice.

As Helena evasively skirted the magnitude of her previous sexual rendezvous with her insatiable God, she blissfully dawned wings and escalated to new heights of achievement in her culinary realm. Her recipes and interlocking rhymes flourished in her backyard garden where the summer sunshine kissed her bare skin and a slight breeze tangled her hair. The foliage and fragrant blossoms that surrounded her nymph-like body, fluttered unpredictably. She scribbled notes with ink on scraps of paper and interspersed the rhetoric with simple, rapidly forged drawings and sketches expressing her increased vitality and imagination.

Helena's garden paradise was abundantly trellised with purple clematis; pale golden honey-suckle; climbing nasturtiums in mango, peach and apple hues; sweet peas in pastel colors; scarlet runner beans; blue moon flowers; lavender cups and saucers; and exotic passion vines.

Below the Goddess was a throng of endless white babies' breath; sapphire lobelia; pink verbena; and canary yellow marigolds, all interplanted with fruit laden orange blossomed zucchini; fiery ripe tomatoes; edible scented herbs; curly lettuce; petite flowered okra; grand thistle headed artichokes; and smooth cool as ice, hidden in the shade, cucumbers.

Helena wanted to gracefully internalize whatever a youthful Diva could creatively justify internalizing during humble preparations for her sacred entry into womanhood by her lover's phallic entity. The naked, nubile Goddess lay on her warm blanket, self absorbed and alone amongst the flora. Serenely and reverently, she rekindled the fond memory and artistry of Napoleon's kisses at the lake, as her fortuitous fingertips trembled lightly across her breasts and bare skin.

With eyes closed toward the brightness of the sun above her, Helena fantasized and deeply internalized her lover as parenthetically as possible by singularly engaging a perfectly suitable elongated fruit between her thighs, thrusting in anticipation of simulated copulative pubescent bliss. With a powerful surge of regenerated longing and lustful abandonment, Helena suddenly froze.

Recalling briefly, the thwarted hen in the henhouse caught in the midst of her private affairs, Helena opened her eyes to Napoleon's unexpected, discreet voice towering high above her. He unabashedly crouched down beside her with the majestic presence of an absolute embodiment and certainly not a figment of her subconscious contemplations. Napoleon removed his clothes and kissed Helena's naked body wherever his lips could plant a kiss, then shyly disengaged the fruit of her interrupted solitary pleasure.

He smiled at her blush of embarrassment, then tenderly inserted his mature, well nurtured and protected, engorged phallus. The pubescent girl was finally a woman embracing the maraca; the barren Goddess was finally the sheath coveting the sword. The stately scepter bearing young man was indeed Helena's rightful, cosmological mate.

Helena wanted to hold Napoleon inside her forever, bear his children and love him beyond infinity. The subsequent tidal wave of frolicking thrusts and ceremonious heaving sanctioned a copious union between friends and lovers, unparalleled in the universe.

A garter snake rustled through the passion vines as the pair of lovers slowly descended from their orgasmic summit, where they willfully tasted the apple. The couple chose banishment over an obscure promise of immortality. Their Eden was complete and unadulterated.

No priest would ever hear whispers of this carnal engagement of betrayal in a confessional. The penance for lost virginity outside of the holy sacrament of matrimony could be eternal and sacrificing another classmate with a humiliating reprimand might be detrimental to Helena's stoic reputation and future heroism.

Poem #5
Companion

I came looking for you in early spring,
But winter still had your chestnut hair

And bronze skin
Somewhere near the sun,

Where ancient breaths hung heavy
With silver jugs and precious stones,

Woven rugs and satin bones.
The tombs, the tombs...

You mustn't go near
Those jeweled high rooms,

Arranged with a feast and a bed,
Content to woo only the dead!

Poem #6
When The Music Comes

Curled up in my woolen shirt
And hand-woven plaid skirt,

I peer at the thin trace
Of sun on a passing face.

I smell the thyme and rosemary
Cooking with the lamb and sherry,

And wonder, as I taste the stew,
Where is the winter keeping you?

Perhaps you sport a furry hat,
And wrap your feet around a cat.

Snow falls white along the path
As I hear water fill the bath.

It makes me want to borrow
Your plans for tomorrow.

Recipe #7
Sumptuous Scallop Soup For Ocean Gurus

-Simmer sliced mushrooms, garlic and whole raw scallops in a pot with olive oil, oyster sauce, cumin, coriander, nutmeg, lime juice, salt, pepper and fenugreek.
-Add wedges of fresh tomato and avocado.
-Heat gently.
-Increase liquids by adding white wine, sour cream and milk.
-Serve with focaccia, cheese wedges, cashews and colorfully dye-stained and peeled boiled eggs nestled among watercress, parsley, black olives and red grapes.

Presentation:
-An indoor greenhouse arrangement amongst exotic flowering vines, tropical birds and darting chameleons will quell anyone's desire to be anywhere else.
-If your mate is delayed by a tornado of trauma and debate, digest your light feast upon a swinging hammock with a preemptive light orgasm of preparatory release.
-Keep the soup warm and your body at ease.
-The wait will be worth the compounded rebate.

Recipe #8
Sumptuous Soup For Beach Lovers

-Prepare a thin tomato cream sauce flavored with cinnamon, lemon, ginger, garlic and dry red wine.
-Add segments of skinless, boneless filleted salmon, tightly curled fiddleheads, cross-sections of morel fungus and greens of young Swiss chard.
-Gently cook and add fresh herbs: sweet marjoram, oregano and basil.
-Serve in festive pottery bowls.
-Float on the surface of each bowl of soup, butter-toasted croutons with a fresh grating of Jarlsburg cheese.
-Enhance a side plate with sourdough bread rolls, cool slices of cantaloupe and long cuttings of Italian parsley.
-Allow the soup to cool, the cheese to melt and the croutons to soften.

Presentation:
-An indoor poolside arrangement amongst potted tropical botanicals will satisfy anyone's naked lust for luxury after a swim.
-Digest your meal in the pool with the one you hastened it for then resonate while copulating underwater like whales mating.

Chapter 5
Not One, But Two Climactic Strategies...
Foie Gras And Caviar

Without any warning, Helena disappeared along with her academic possessions and personal belongings. At her tender age, she hadn't accumulated any wealth, only a basket of precious odds and ends: colorful small stones, iridescent clamshells, strings of dried berry necklaces, and a few sentimental gifts of admiration from transient foreign classmates studying at the girls' Academy on student visas. A suitcase held her clothing, sketchbooks, diaries, toiletries and collection of non-redeemable treasures and trinkets. The remaining cache of resourceful tools and strategies, and the creative language skills that she developed as a means of communication and survival, were in her head.

Helena was AWOL. She eloped with her Napoleon to places far beyond her backyard and kitchen where she began to ascertain the meaning of life. Her disappearance caused suspicion but not much alarm. She didn't request parental endorsement and wasn't surprised when they disapproved of her plans. They wanted her to marry a country boy, not a college student with a dream to pursue a professional career. Nor was she concerned that her parents neglected an offering in the form of a blessing or monetary endowment. A blessing would have been hypocritical and a dowry would have threatened her sense of liberty. She had grown accustomed to their obscure prejudices throughout her youth and now she was diligently prepared to reject their lifestyle, indoctrinations and beliefs at a full estimated cost of total banishment.

Helena's desires for the world outside of her home and school were well known to her female classmates destined for idleness and her female teachers sworn to chaste lives celebrating the Holy Eucharist like a weekly lobster-fest by the sea. Speaking in garbled, irrational tongues at prayer meetings, they attempted to impress the feeble girls already destined for a celibate or lesbian life at the convent. The nuns at Helena's school were spiritually married to Jesus and physically wedded to each other. They were determined to embridle even the most cynical pubescent rebels like Helena.

With the mounting pressure to become catastrophically converted, Helena jumped the fence. Like a gazelle in the wild, she eloquently raised her head to the wind and escaped a destiny meant for the lame stragglers unenviably tethered to lives of prayer, forever kissing the feet of the elevated, painted-plaster-cast corpse of sweet Jesus in the convent chapel. Internal suffering and torment, penance and sacrifice pursued them as they mindlessly rocked and rubbed themselves against the pews for nearly effortlessly induced orgasms.

The nuns' prayers were always answered, they told the girls. Of course they never revealed the secret contents of their devout requests. Only the staggered and undisguised stupors following their holy conversations with God unveiled their masked enterprises. Helena deduced that a nun's orgasms were misinterpreted to be manifestations of the Lord empowering them with the spiritual strength to preach the holy word. The internal shudders, quakes and sexual exhaustion were ultimately worth their cloistered lives, it seemed.

Most speculated, some questioned and a few disbelieved Helena's informal exit. The valiant Goddess was galloping with her fearless Napoleon, high astride Wagram, his gray Arabian steed. In reality, she was in exile, residing in a clear dimension, devoting her time and energy to the writing of her first book.

Helena's fascination for food preparation traveled with her, but her poetry compositions subsided as prose creation dominated and sex with Napoleon flourished day and night. Living with Napoleon was a closely treasured dream of Helena's that finally materialized. Sleeping and waking with her lover, jogging, cycling, dining and relaxing with him, consecrated the affair. In essence, she was Napoleon's bride and he was her eternal companion.

Now that Helena attained new status, it was time for her to incorporate components from her intriguing, urban environment. With an ambiance of warm candlelight, gold rings of endowment on their fingers and a bottle of Champagne, the mated pair christened their primitive redwood dining table with a jovial toast of marital confirmation and eternal happiness. Delicate servings of fresh baked sourdough bread crowned with warm slices of port-marinated, garlic-encrusted, peach-glazed, roasted foie gras hailed the beginning of their lives together. A second, but no less satiable manna was another fresh baked bread that Helena flavored with whole caraway seeds. Small thick slices were then dominated with mounds of caviar sprinkled with Feta cheese and piquant ruddy hued olives.

The festive proclamation of their common table evolved into a prolonged petting and kissing celebration within the entire one room high-rise apartment. Their shared foie gras and caviar communion led to fornication among the hanging and climbing potted epiphytes that surrounded the silk clad floor mattress.

Their playful relations and intervals of love making transpired again and again; their frolicking in and out of states of ecstasy while eating, kissing, fondling, and sucking grew enhanced by nibbling the last and final bits of everything edible, drinkable and pleasurable. Not one fragment of foie gras or caviar, drop of wine or excretion of bodily nectar remained unconsumed.

By day, the tiny elevated abode in the clouds became the two lovers' precious garden paradise with sunshine cascading through large windows sustaining an indoor jungle of exotic blossoms. By night, moonlight trickled over the lovers' glistening bare skin as they sprawled, exhausted and asleep among tangled sheets in the darkness of the cool, sweet scented orchid air.

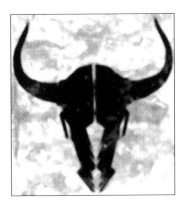

Poem #7
First Nightmare

Something in the wind
Is causing me to weaken.
The ocean sends me
From her shore;
The setting sun beckons
Me to her red door.

Are you somewhere in the snow
Or somewhere in between?
Do you still lament in
Autumn's glowing harbor,
Washing in the rainwater,
Crying like a crow?

My search for you
Employs the murky day.
I scan the seaside,
Listen for your voice
In the empty shells, and follow
Footpaths in the sand.

I stumble across strange faces
And rush through secret places,
Wondering how long you've slept
In this narrow bed, wearing
Clothes you do not own?
Come out of your simple home.

Your voice is quiet as the rain.
I cannot hear you through
The windowpane. You're looking underfed.
Let me bring you tea with honey.
Whispers and the sound of tears
Falling in my bowl,

Wind and the sound of waves
Crashing, drown my soul.
Parting without a poem or sweetened bread
Is more sad than seabirds dying,
And all the yarrows
Trying to prophesy alone.

Recipe #9
Goddess's Rapture Rampant With Aroma

-Rub olive oil, salt and pepper inside the cavities of halved and seeded acorn squash.

-Stuff the first half of the squash with raw scallops in a marinade of garlic, licorice liqueur, white wine, cream, butter and lemon.

-Crown this half with an oiled and seasoned whole portabella mushroom cap.

-Stuff the second half of the squash with cubed zucchini, tomatoes, onions, grated cheeses and raw sunflower seeds.

-Crown the second half with an oiled and seasoned whole portabella mushroom cap.

-Bake for thirty minutes at 400 degrees or until the mushrooms appear roasted and the contents under the caps are steaming and tender.

-Place the mushroom caps on slices of herb bread and serve the squash halves on a bed of Jasmine rice embellished with large, edible, orange squash blossoms.

Presentation:

-Commemorate the end of summer with an autumn colored tablecloth decked with a seasonal basket of colorfully textured decorative gourds and small pumpkins for immediate visual flair and later winter use.

-A comforting pot of chamomile tea with honey should provide a relaxing setting for discussions of historic significance.

Recipe #10
Basmati Banquet With Rabbit and Deer

-Simmer rabbit breasts and thighs in sweet sherry, dry red wine and sweet hot mango chutney.

-Add to the simmer, venison sausages.

-Steam in the same pot with the wild meats: okra, snap peas, mushrooms, zucchini, carrots, assorted sweet peppers, small onions, sliced dried apricots and prunes.

-Add garlic, cloves, cardamom, crushed chili peppers, fenugreek, curry, cumin and a generous addition of coconut milk.

-Stir and simmer until liquids reduce and thicken.

-Serve on a generous bed of Basmati rice cooked with saffron and fresh coriander.

-Garnish the meal with maroon-centered pale yellow okra blossoms.

-Augment the dish with a yogurt/cucumber/apple salad, boasting a lavish scattering of blue starflowers.

-Provide crisp breads on the side and a large pot of strong coffee.

Presentation:

-Serve the meal on a yellow tablecloth with a vase of fragrant purple lilacs.

-This aromatically stimulating feast might keep you and your guests up late.

-Be prepared to engage in a lengthy boisterous evening of chatter and chess matches.

Chapter 6
Halving The Avocado For The Seed

Following a sprightly morning jaunt to the market in the fall, Helena returned to her high-rise apartment with a knapsack of treasures. Her Napoleon was attending university classes and wouldn't arrive until early evening.

Helena usually spent her days in bookstores and libraries, then returned to her lofty apartment where she immersed herself in her writing and cooked whatever luxuriously tempting delicacies inspired her taste buds and sensual appetite.

Fortunately for Helena, Napoleon was not difficult to stimulate, surprise or please. Navigating his emotional territory by her instinctive impulses became an exciting avenue for Helena to explore. Her imagination, enthusiasm and fondness for natural beauty was graciously rewarded by Napoleon's supplanting his Goddess with occasional love tokens of amber, turquoise, and pearls.

She enjoyed sequestering random opportunities for isolated activities unfamiliar to her. Some days she explored the art galleries and museums and other days she frequented the campus swimming pool and sauna with a friend she met at the library. Clarise was her name, and she too was writing a book.

Helena emptied her knapsack on the redwood table. She had ventured to the market alone that morning and bought two ripe mangos, six avocados, fresh sour cream, a vial of saffron and a smooth pale green jade object d' art. The life size oriental jade phallus was an ornamental embellishment that Helen was sure would make a marvelous centerpiece for her avocado salad.

The ornament's intended function could be hedonistically applied to lovemaking with Napoleon during or after dinner, conjured Helena. In addition she thought, a naked tribal dance accompanied by musical drumming preceding the tropical meal, could be an enchanting way to begin the evening.

The effervescent Helena began food preparations immediately, halving the avocados and setting aside the inner seeds. She spooned the mature green avocado flesh into a beautiful red glazed ceramic platter. Ripe slices of golden mango were added. A generous squeeze of lemon and a splash of white wine baptized the ingredients.

With a careful toss to mingle them, the mango and avocado were harmoniously intermixed and ready for a lavish topping of sour cream accentuated by a delicate orange scattering of saffron. At the center of the abundantly filled pottery dish, Helena firmly erected the jade ornament in a central upright position with a forceful plunge into the salad. At the base of the pinnacle, Helena arranged huge deep pink and brilliant yellow hibiscus blossoms.

The semi precious phallus stood in place exceptionally well, exhibiting its remarkably detailed external carvings. The entire dish was a stage of erotic splendor and charm.

It was seven o'clock and time for the feast to begin. Helena's lover would accompany her any minute. She placed her coquettish creation on the redwood table, lit a candle then flooded the room with recorded percussive sounds. She shed her clothes and began dancing to the strong rhythmic beating of drums. Helena was ready for Napoleon to arrive.

Her dancing acquired a vibrant frenzy of sexually symbolic movements when Napoleon expectedly entered the house of rapture he formerly knew to be his quiet apartment. The two male friends who were with Napoleon were also expected, but Helena had totally forgotten. She paused abruptly and stood naked and motionless in the flickering candlelight. Panting slightly, she desperately wondered why she didn't remember their casual dinner plans with guests that evening. She didn't know how she would explain her lack of attire or the phallus in the salad.

Napoleon acknowledged Helena's glitch in her memory; with a pitiable grin, he apologized for not calling to remind her of their plans. Unable to withhold a chuckle, he reached for her clothes and kissed her as he caught sight of the dildo-decorated salad.

Helena calmly dressed and announced with a confident simulation of a cordial smile, that dinner would be in twenty minutes. With little space in which to maneuver in the dim light, Helena masterfully tossed a towel over the salad before her guests had a chance to notice the questionably decorated entrée.

She had previously met Napoleon's histology classmates and noticed at the time, their apparent introversion and lack of humor. She knew that Napoleon found them intellectually and conversationally interesting and assumed that he probably wasn't aware of their sullen unresponsiveness.

Feeling somewhat flustered, embarrassed and purely mortified, the Queen of Cock-Ups quietly begged Napoleon to telephone order a pizza while she attended to the avocado seeds at the sink. They needed to be suspended in containers of water to aid sprouting. The seeds would eventually become regal fruit bearing trees for her sun drenched apartment plantation of tropical botanicals. Somehow, salvaging the avocado seeds at this very moment in time felt like a desperately necessary compensatory act of reconciliation that simply could not justify a delay.

Helena distractedly transferred the camouflaged salad to the refrigerator. Eventually, the arrival of a deluxe pizza salvaged the unforeseen, cataclysmic situation. The bewildered students hastily concluded the dining experience in a serious attempt to recover their senses and deny their shyness, as the speechless semi-clad writer attempted to rescue her self-respect and eradicate her indiscretion.

When the guests left, the drumming resumed and the salacious salad reoccupied the tabletop. Helena and Napoleon sedated themselves in each other's teasing and laughter. After a generous sharing of wine, with clumsy unsteadiness they undressed each other then glutinously devoured the obscenely exotic cacophony of unyielding, delightful flavors comprising the meal.

Napoleon daringly admired the craftsmanship of the hand carved, smooth, pale green jade penis still decorating the center of the empty serving dish. He playfully caressed the object in his hand then slowly guided it between Helena's intoxicated thighs as she poignantly tucked the pink and yellow hibiscus in her head of frazzled sun streaked hair. Napoleon's own jealously throbbing phallic piece found its way to his lover's sultry wet mouth.

Following Helena's simple lack of attention to earlier dining detail, the unanticipated falter at the alter of the distracted decadent Diva, would soon be forgotten. The lustful evening of lovemaking was merely beginning. Between uncountable bursts of orgasmic crescendos and embarrassing cries of sustained humiliation, Helena deservedly submitted to a climactic over-indulgence of emotional and physical restoration, regardless of its transitory satisfaction; her concern did not extend beyond the crucial moment.

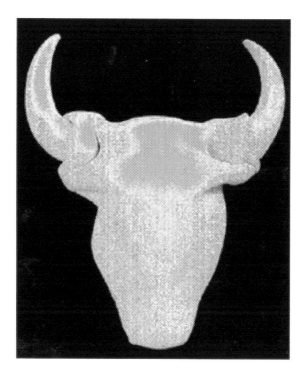

Poem #8
Dream At Petty Harbor

At the edge of my country
I beckoned the sun.

She climbed out of her ocean bed,
Red faced and anxious to run

With the puffins and gulls
To your bedside.

I should have left with the tide,
Instead of the rising one.

With the ferry run aground
And the migrant birds in sight,

I counted a few red leaves
Scattered absently around

The wharf, and pretended
That I was on my way to your house,

When actually I was looking
For a place to spend the night.

A sagging bed and feather quilt
Seduced me Island style,

As the seafaring Morduns kept me
As their daughter for a while.

They were like penguins
Shuffling across the sand,

An old seaman and his bride
Shipwrecked in their shanty.

The salt encrusted ancient home
Gripped the stony shore;

Enduring centuries, it bore
The Viking doors and pantry.

You should have been there
Bent over with your height,

Warmed by smoky oil lamps
And glinting candlelight.

You would have eaten ocean cod
And oversized potatoes,

While stooping under Viking ceilings,
Dining at a wooden table.

You should have been there;
I missed you through the night

When the Screech brought out
The Maritime tales,

And the flaccid bed held only
My horns and plaintiff wails.

Your naked feet would not have fit
Beneath the antique covers;

Our hammock-cradled bodies would have
Clung like marooned lovers,

Stranded on an Island
For a night of autumn gales.

The feather quilt and swaying bed
Engaged me until dawn,

When upon the ship again,
I found the Island gone.

My pocket held two farewell gifts
Of prehistoric charm,

A seashell and a rock
Worn smooth by stormy weather.

A sailor I was never meant to be,
Acquainted with the tides

And buried treasure;
I sighed as I finally sensed

My journey's seasick end,
But welcomed nothing else

Than returning to your shore
For endless pleasure.

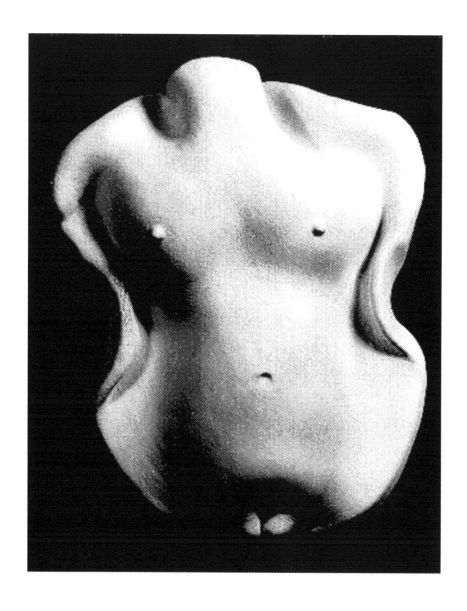

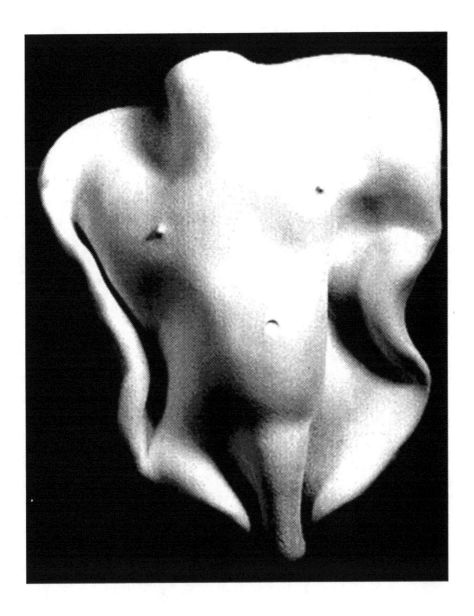

Recipe #11
Sweet Fruit Rice Wraps

-Pre-cook Jasmine rice with sugar, cinnamon, nutmeg and cardamom.
-Stir in dried cranberries and prepared vanilla custard to thicken the rice mixture.
-Add long strips of peeled apples, mangoes and bananas sprinkled with orange liqueur.
-Fill soft wrappers with thick layers of the rice mixture and flavored fruit.
-Bake them at 325 degrees for twenty minutes.
-Take this opportunity to engage in mischievous kitchen foreplay with your lover in preparation for the delightful culinary reward.
-Retrieve the warm wraps from the oven when heated through, or when you and your mate have sufficiently exhausted your favorite acts of sensual arousal.
-Lavish the wraps with maple syrup and whipped cream.

Presentation:
-Enjoy your elevated pre-orgasmic states while dining on the prepared appetizing preliminaries.
-To sustain the delay between the sweet and following savory edibles, dine at a table draped in a highly distracting, intricately woven lace cloth with fragrant pink rose petals scattered about.

Recipe #12
Savory Salmon Wraps

-Pre-cook rice with soy sauce, oyster sauce, garlic and ginger.
-Toss the rice with flaked pre-cooked salmon.
-Top with pepper strips, asparagus, onions and a sprinkle of white wine.
-Fill wrappers with the rice and salmon mixture.
-Top with creamy cucumber-yogurt and sun-dried tomato dressings.
-Add a layer of Jarlsberg cheese slices.
-Roll up the wrappers and bake them at 325 degrees.
-Take this opportunity to engage in mischievous kitchen sex with your lover in expectation of a sudden increase in appetites for a doubly delightful culinary reward.
-Retrieve the warm wraps from the oven when they are hot and steaming, or when you and your mate have sufficiently exhausted your favorite positions and attained heights of menacing ecstasy.

Presentation:
-Enjoy your elevated post-orgasmic states while dining on the prepared follow-up conclusions.
-Treat yourselves to two or more wraps each and a relaxing pot of herbal tea.
-Bring the meal to a close with a gratuitous nap in the sunshine.

Excerpt From Helena's Book: The Three Sisters
Excerpt 1: The Slaughter

Arranged like a Triangle of Adorable Cherubs in pink flannel pajamas, six-year-old Bonky, seven-year-old Shanty and eight-year-old Windy slept tangled under a cloud of white bed sheets and a billowy star patterned patchwork quilt. For lack of space and wealth, they still shared the same enigmatic bed they had since the beginning of time.

Their communal center of government was snuggly nested on the lofty second floor of a farmhouse, under the attic window where observations of the outside world were considerably expansive. The children's elevated view of the empire meant that everything occurring outside could be seen, heard or speculated upon from their Tower of Youthful Wisdom and Tribal Order.

The small attic room was littered with clothes, toys, dolls, books, paper, other school paraphernalia and a few musical instruments.

A cockerel strutted outside under the attic window and crowed in jubilant bursts as the sun appeared on a flat stretch of prairie horizon. The flamboyant feathered alarm awakened Windy. She jolted out of her dreams and cried to her siblings, "Wake up! Wake up, or we'll miss it!"

Shanty groggily stirred and chirped, "Yeah, I don't want to miss this!"

From Windy's hierarchical position at the head of the bed, she administered an inaugural shove with her foot to the insubordinate slumbering Bonky, who was inverted under the covers at the foot of the bed. "Come on Bonky. This is the day!" reminded Windy.

Bonky lazily rolled over. From the neighboring position next to her, Shanty pushed Bonky with her feet until she rolled her right off the bed. With a thump and a snore, Bonky continued sleeping on the floor.

Desperate to begin the day, Windy crawled out of bed and slipped the straps of an accordion over her shoulders. Within seconds, the Grand

Master of Torture and Interrogation exploded forth a loud and lively tune as she heaved the bellows back and forth in rhythmic syncopation.

The instrument's keys and chords issued a metronomically regulated acoustic sound that caused Bonky to unequivocally end her peaceful slumber. She jumped up off the floor and quickly scrambled into her clothes. She yelled at her tormentor, "Put that thing down! I'm getting up already! I'm getting up!"

Shanty covered her ears tightly with her hands just as Windy abruptly abandoned her weapon. Within minutes, all three Storm Troopers were dressed and ready to harness the day.

"I wonder who will be first: John, Paul, George or Ringo?" queried wide-eyed Bonky.

Shanty replied, "It hardly matters. They're all doomed!"

On their anxious way out, each of the girls hastily ingested their usual morning breakfasts of puffed wheat, sweetened with heaping teaspoons of sugar and soaked in reservoirs of fresh cow's milk. When they were finished, Windy gave the usual, "On your mark. Get set. Go!" routine for any opportunity that required speed or urgency, as this one did.

With uncombed curls and stringy locks of sun-bleached hair in ocher, sienna and shades of umber, the team of sprinters raced outside past the crowing rooster until they reached the wooden fence surrounding the pigpen. They climbed to the top of the three-tiered enclosure and with attempted composure, clumsily arranged themselves in a row. Their primitive stadium seating required much conscientious steadying and balancing to prevent an unintended fall.

The athletes' Father and owner of the farmland, was already inside the pen holding his shotgun. He was waiting for the pigs: John, George, Paul and Ringo to settle down following their sudden burst of activity, which seemed to coincide with the arrival of the fans.

"Go back to the house! You little monkeys shouldn't be out here!" ordered the Farmer with a distinct tone of exasperation and annoyance in his voice.

The girls shouted in accidental harmony and unison, "But dad! Yesterday you said we could watch if we were quiet."

"Alright, alright! But don't make me change my mind," warned the Farmer. The on-looking groupies became dead silent and the quartet of hefty boars settled. The full grown band of soon to be evolved pork chops was once a newly arrived set of affectionately named quadruplets, wrapped in dolls' blankets and bottle fed in the arms of their adoptive and nurturing child hosts.

For two years the pseudo-parents contributed to the daily fattening of the venerated Squadron of Prisoners despite their somewhat punishable past histories including: John's attempted escape while rooting for the elusive truffle that never was on the other side of the fence; Paul's misconduct when he impregnated a neighbor's sow while on parole; Georges' deceptive back scratching against the lower boards of the pig barn until the entire structure lost its support and tumbled to the ground; and Ringo's ill-mannered, unremorseful, carnivorous consumption of Hercules, Bonky's favorite stuffed teddy bear that horrifyingly tumbled out of her arms and into the pigpen just before feeding time one morning. The only remaining scrap of the revered bear was his podgy tail, unsalvageable from the mud and dung that gradually buried the trophy.

All four of the Death Row Inmates stood fastidious and motionless in a queue. They starred straight at the Trio of Enemy Accomplices positioned for duty on the fence. Periodically, the mesmerized corn-fed, pink-skinned, musician-anointed swine snorted and oinked, melodically.

Inside the fence at the feet of the patient wardens, the Executioner slowly lowered himself on one knee and held the shotgun in place. Unimpaired by physical or emotional strain, he took aim and fired. George went down with a violent squeal. Blood poured out of the hole in his forehead. John, Paul and Ringo raced wildly in circles inside the confines of the pen. The resolute fans smiled magnanimously and gloated over their anticipated favorite cuts of grilled, stewed or boiled pork.

Windy staked a hurried claim, "I want the ears, simmered with onions!"

Shanty hollered, "I'll take the hooves, stewed with mushrooms!"

And Bonky covetously piped, "I have to have the tail, grilled with cheese!"

The Farmer ignored the frantic display of the remaining livestock. With a large butcher's knife in his hand, he approached George lying on his side. He grasped the dead hog by the snout, then sliced George's throat to enable the necessary rapid escape of blood.

Bonky mumbled with tears in her eyes, "I guess that's one down and three to go."

The Farmer dragged the carcass by the hind legs to the curing rack. He tied a thick rope to George's hind ankles and suspended him upside down from the top horizontal wood beam. With a steady outstretched finger pointed at the hanging carcass, Windy surmised, "That's a lot of bacon!"

Shanty and Bonky nodded in agreement from their stadium seats. The Farmer returned to death row. It was evident that his Petite Accomplices were eager to continue the survival of their own intelligent dominant species.

This time Ringo became the motionless but grunting target for the predictably perfect shot. The enterprising Killer once again dropped to his knee and took aim. His years of experience defending his agricultural domain, made a mockery of his passive target. Ringo went down like an enemy surveying the fort.

"Should we play drums for him?" asked Windy.

"No way!" said Bonky, "The accordion this morning was bad enough!"

"Besides, George didn't get a musical send off," interrupted Shanty.

With a slightly delayed response to Bonky's curse of the accordion, Windy pushed and shoved Bonky until she lost her balance and fell to the ground from her prestigious perch. Bonky started to howl.

"Settle down," warned the Executioner again, "if you don't behave, you will all have to go back to the house."

Windy pulled Bonky back onto the fence. Bonky repositioned herself and stopped howling. Shanty leaned toward Bonky and whispered, "We don't want to miss this. It's very educational." Bonky and Windy nodded in agreement.

They could see that Ringo was now hanging from the rafter next to George. The remaining pigs, Paul and John, were extremely restless from the two previous slayings. The deadly shots seemed to buckle and soil the atmosphere with an unforgivable smell of exsanguinations and fresh excrement.

The Slayer was restless as well, and was unable to establish proper aim for either remaining target. An idea besieged the Farmer's intellect. "Windy, bring the accordion out here. A little music might calm them down," suggested the King of the Jungle and Lord of All Beasts.

"Oh, crap!" groaned Shanty and Bonky, as they eyed their Father who stood in direct earshot of their voices.

Windy bounded off the fence. As she ran back to the house, she shouted, " I'll play a ballad. That should work!" The Gymnast wasted no time as she stumbled back to the pigpen with the accordion strapped to her chest. She gracefully lumbered up to her place at the top of the fence and began to play.

Shanty and Bonky covered their ears with their hands. The agitated pigs began to calm down. Paul and John stoically joined ranks, side by side. They stood perfectly still and starred straight at the Executioner's

Daughter, daunted by the hypnotic tune she continued to tirelessly propel forth from the bellows of the music box.

Windy's Father dropped into position for the third shot. Paul went down. The remaining John, squealed helplessly as he raced around the inside of the pen, alone and hysterical. He frantically kicked up dirt and fecal mess as he recklessly slammed his heavy body against the wooden fence. Windy stopped playing the ballad and instead, bellowed forth a jaunty Marching tune.

The Farmer slit Paul's throat and dragged him out of the pen to suspend him from the rafter, next to Ringo and George. In spite of Windy's musical distraction, John refused to compose himself. Without the companionship of a single teammate, his behavior was suddenly erratic and unpredictable.

Shanty and Bonky yelled at Windy, "Stop that racket!" But, Windy just played louder and faster than before. Consequently, John squealed louder and louder and ran faster and faster around the inside of the pen until finally with a crack and a snap, the delinquent boar broke through the fence and scurried off through the barnyard and across the field toward the bush.

"Shit! Alright Windy, that's enough!" complained the Farmer. Windy immediately stopped playing. Shanty and Bonky uncovered their ears.

Bonky quietly mimicked her Father, "Shit! Thank goodness!"

Realizing that a pig on the loose was potentially any neighbor's food for the winter, the Executioner swung his rifle over his shoulder and headed in the direction of the escapee. The Farmer's task was now that of a sniper. He would not return from the woods, or the dark of night, or the glow of dawn unless John's carcass accompanied him.

As the Sniper headed off on his solitary mission, he gave no specific instructions to his three impetuous daughters. He knew they were afraid of the dark and wouldn't dare follow him.

67

As expected, the Little Prison Guards deserted their official seats and headed back toward the house. Shanty and Bonky scampered ahead while Windy eloquently rendered a mournful tune on the accordion. She plodded after her sisters, purposefully stepping in time to the ponderous requiem that intoxicated the atmosphere with an accomplished, electrifying distant charm.

Poem #9
Summer's End

Miss autumn climbs my noble tree
To castle heights where winds blow free.

Among the princess-hair-like leaves
With fibers gold, she slowly weaves

And eats the scepter gold pear fruit
While humming soft as Pan's reed flute,

When on the pasture lands Pan sought
The evening comfort of his flock.

Recipe #13
Jellied Pigs' Feet For Sprinters

-Soak in cold water for two hours: cleaned butcher-prepared pig's feet and cuttings of fresh sage, rosemary and thyme.
-Add whole cloves of garlic, whole onions, whole clove spice, cinnamon sticks, nutmeg, salt and black peppercorns.
-Simmer for two hours or until the meat falls off the anklebones and spices infuse the air.
-Cool the contents, then strain the liquids from the solids.
-Separate the meat from all the other ingredients.
-Recombine the meat with the strained aromatic liquid in a decorative serving bowl.
-Stir the contents to distribute them evenly.
-Garnish with mint leaves.
-Refrigerate overnight so that the contents will gel.

Presentation:
-Serve with sweetened fresh basil lemonade, chilled with pre-frozen whole seedless green grapes, instead of ice-cubes.
-Round out the cool entree with caraway seed bread, orbs of Bocconcini cheese, and ripe quartered apples, pears and pomegranates.
-This is best consumed after a quick sprint in hot weather.

Recipe #14:
Eulogy To A Pig

-Fill pork heart ventricles with garlic, small onions and truffles.
-Place the stuffed heart in a slurry of dry red wine, sweet red sherry, apple juice, cloves, cinnamon sticks, nut meg and bay leaves.
-Occasionally, roll the heart around in its juices during roasting.
-Bake for one half hour at 400 degrees.
-Surround the heart with carrots, potatoes, scarlet runner beans, brussel sprouts and yams bathed lightly in olive oil.
-Bake another half hour or until the vegetables are tender and lightly browned, and the liquids are reduced.
-Praise the sacrificed pig with a reminiscence and grateful account of its significance to the food chain:

Upon this dish
I will impart
A trifle bit
Of candor;

Before I chose
The tender pork,
I nearly cooked
A gander.

Presentation:
-Invite your sweetheart to this dinner on Valentine's Day.
-Begin serving the meal with a kiss, a box of cherry chocolates, and an armful of red roses.
-Follow the dinner with a vigorous uninhibited floundering in the nearest bed, like piglets wallowing in the mud.
-The white cloth covered dining table flaunting heart shaped cupid-darted cookies on a plate, may be temporarily abandoned until the grunts and groans of fornication emitted from the small, but convenient bed in the den, rescind, and the post coital temptations of the palates resume their courtship where they started.

Variation:
-Simmer chicken feet in sweet soy sauce, white grape juice, Teriyaki garlic sauce, white wine, plum sauce, ginger and mango chutney.
-Add partially cooked rice, sugar-snap-peas, shitake mushrooms and whole baby corn to the pot.
-Simmer until the rice is fully cooked and your neighbor's rooster crows frantically.
-Provide a ceramic, bird shaped bowl for holding discarded, nibbled clean, ankle and toe bones.

Presentation:
-Serve yourself and amenable guests on no particular occasion.
-If guests bring other food, all-the-better for those who love to orally challenge gelatinous digits of fowl origins.
-Arrange a table with stately carved and painted wooden chickens on a red-and-white-striped tablecloth.
-Conversations might revolve around henhouses and space flight.

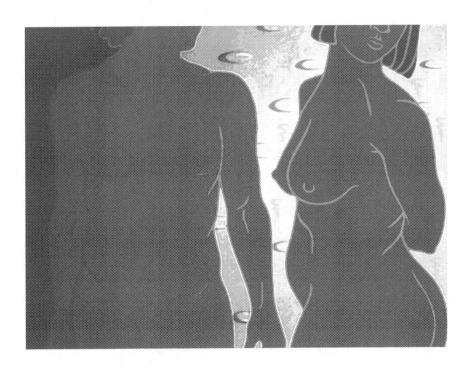

Chapter 7
Seduction Of The Long-Legged Alaskan King Crab

Helena's enthusiasm, spontaneity and curiosity were beginning to fade. She started spending more time writing and less time seeking sexual pleasure and culinary success. If she took a day off now it was to shop for canned sardines, cheese spread, sliced bread, apples and chocolate bars. Tropical fruits and vegetables, dairy products, herbs, spices and imported ornaments were no longer on her list of necessary or even desirable items. Helena resorted to ordering in Fast Food at a twice-weekly rate.

Coincidentally, Helena and Napoleon seemed to make love only twice a week as well and only on weekends, a major decline from once, twice or three times daily. She wondered if it was a consequence of excessive work and stress, she being a dedicated writer and Napoleon being a full time student. Or could it be the residual morbid fumes that emanated from Napoleon's lungs three times a week following anatomy classes designed for students living in solitary confinement, dating only on weekends. The essence of formaldehyde embalming fluid and notable decay of the offending in-class cadaver saturated a student's breathing apparatus with ghastly persistence. The resulting deathly odor subsided only long enough to make love twice consecutively, and from the stern to avoid excessive mouth contact, otherwise affectionately known as kissing.

After much psychoanalytical thought and a few discussions with Clarise at the library, Helena decided that it was a corpse-like fatigue syndrome affecting their lives. She and Napoleon were always tired, overworked and feeling slightly nauseated.

Clarise and her female companion on the other hand, lived in full vivacious lesbian fashion, kissing each other at street corners, on the subway, and in the parks. Neither of them suffered from fatigue or disinterest in anything. Clarise was a sophisticated, socially respectable, proudly declared highly orgasmic linguist and already twice published novelist. Her lover was a cellist in the university symphony orchestra. Helena recognized the rule of Lesbos in their eyes before they even kissed in front of her.

Compared to the half-hideous, groping, pretentious lesbian classmates from Helena's past life at the convent, Clarise and her lover appeared to be living monuments of a dignified anthropologically and culturally inspired phenomenon deeply rooted in ancient civilization. They were definitely Goddesses. Helena felt immensely humbled by her friends' apparent abilities to achieve success and contentment.

She thoughtfully decided that an intense phase of sexual stimulation might reawaken her inner desire and enthusiasm for love. An orgasmic cycle began with a frequency and furry that shocked Helena herself. Her fixation and freedom to climax with or without Napoleon, with or without objects, lubricants, rubber things that squeaked or didn't, metal wands that vibrated or wouldn't, became a minor obsession for the wanton sex Goddess to research in depth.

For Napoleon, Helena's intensive blitzkrieg of self-gratification became a very regular and highly anticipated form of entertainment, sometimes passive and sometimes mutually interactive, depending on Napoleon's degree of wakefulness or fatigue. Either way, Helena and Napoleon regained their internal sense of vibrancy and vigor at a very economical price, emotionally and physically.

Napoleon's dubious anatomy classes finally ended and new studies occupied him irresistibly, as Helena's manuscript equally possessed her. Each of them exhibited dynamic resourcefulness and dedication to their work without continuing to sacrifice their most basic passionate longing for each other.

As Helena's writing progressed, she realized that her sexual appetite was near saturation, but her craving for epicurean fare was sadly unfulfilled beyond recognition. Her meager wiry frame was not without warmth; it was simply without sustenance. Gaunt, was not a becoming feature of any young Goddess or thriving young woman in her twenties, Helena decided. The sardine and apple diet would have to cease.

Helena dreamily summoned the culinary Gods and Goddesses to her redwood table and sobbed over her lack of new recipes and disparaging disinterest in hearty or festive preparations. She worried that her Napoleon was a bit thin too, and wondered how she could have lost her penchant for cooking, her appetite for consumption and her interest in hosting petit banquets.

After a reflective rummage through her accumulated sketches and poetic notations, Helena considered a cure for her troubles. It was time for a memorable feast. Napoleon's birthday was at the end of the week. Helena decided they would celebrate the occasion at someone else's expense of exertion in order to recover her own absent sense of effort. She quickly made reservations at a small, quaint seafood restaurant nearby.

Helena was absolutely determined to challenge her lover to an oral seduction of the long, sweet, succulent legs of an Alaskan King Crab. What could be more satisfying than an undertaking to reflect upon the divine and the sublime? What could be more arousing than such a tantalizing feast with candlelight and wine? Helena swooned at the mere thought of offering her lover the inner white thighs of a steamy, garlic butter dipped crustacean that once roamed the seabed. And she was sure a sumptuous dessert would persuade her to revitalize the culinary refinement within her.

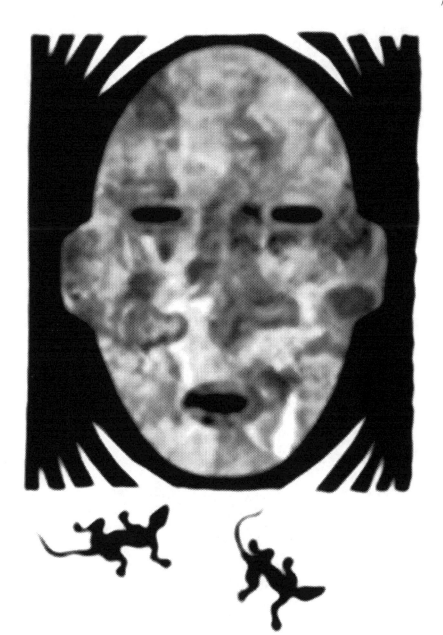

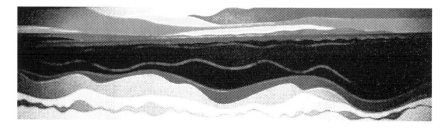

Poem #10
Second Nightmare

The ocean is a deep blueness
Between us,

Too rough to sail ships across,
Too rugged on the shores

For walking in bare feet.
Curled naked against

An ancient stone
I lament in my sleep.

The eternal sound of the sea,
Loud and soft,

Tumbles ferociously now,
Then slips quietly back

To another tumble.
It rises and falls,

Swells and sinks
In a great circle of

Sky and sand.
My face becomes salt,

Sucking the sea stones,
Swaying with the tide,

Roaring, shuffling, breathing,
Constantly heaving

Until I am the sea,
Salty, surging, roaring,

Slipping over rocks,
Clattering on the shore.

Recipe #15
Snails, Bread and Tails To Entice The Timid

-In a roasting pan, place raw snails with olive oil, cracked black pepper, crushed garlic, sliced mushrooms, chopped peeled tomatoes, tomato sauce, barbecue sauce, sweet hot mango chutney, chili sauce, curry paste, soy sauce, sweet marjoram, thyme, sage, dry red wine and sweet sherry.
-Stir together.
-Bake in an oven uncovered at 450 degrees for approximately one hour or until juices are well reduced and snails are grilled in appearance.
-Stir the contents intermittently.
-Taste for perfection and adjust flavors if necessary.
-Sprinkle with grated Parmesan cheese, crumbled Feta cheese and chopped sweet basil.
-Serve hot on fresh baked thick slices of bread.
-Follow with a crisp spinach salad consisting of peeled wedges of oranges, sliced cucumber, broccoli and rounds of cantaloupe.
-Toss with sweetened orange juice and Balsamic Vinaigrette.
-Add a heavy grating of Parmesan, Asiago and Feta cheese.
-Garnish with sliced black olives.
-Cover the entire top surface of the salad with chilled, cooked and shelled tiger shrimp and lobster tails.

-Add a squeeze of lemon and ground pepper.
-Pour a sweet creamy anise dressing over the seafood.

Presentation:
-Consider these to be appetizers that don't require a meal to follow.
-Serve on a marble tabletop with a vase of white peonies and fern fronds.
-Glasses of red and white wine might suitably escort the snails and tails.
-As bare buttocks and forearms connect with the coolness of marble, and muzzles inhale the spicy scent of peonies, a spontaneous engagement of thrusting force will give fresh meaning to already mature adventures.

Excerpt From Helena's Book: The Three Sisters
Excerpt 2: The Beheadings

In their messy moonlit bedroom, Windy, Shanty and Bonky slept like vampire bats after a blood-fest. It was an hour before sunrise when their alarm clock clanged, mercilessly. They knew the roosters would still be sleeping this early.

Bonky bolted upright and yelled, "Let those heads roll!"

Shanty sat up and remarked, "They won't roll. They will just drop off."

Windy climbed out of bed and correctly added, "What matters is that their heads still squawk, even after they have fallen to the ground!"

"Their voice boxes still have air in them and if you give their throats a little push with a stick, they squawk."

"Neat-Oh," cried Bonky.

The Trinity of Terror rushed into their day clothes, skipped breakfast and ran out of the sleepy house in the twilight toward the barnyard where the day's beheadings were scheduled to occur. Eight roosters were still sleeping on the lower branches of the maple trees, but the carnage had already begun.

Two roosters' heads were camped on the ground at the base of a bloody tree stump where the girls' Father embedded the sharp edge of an axe blade, the handle poised for re-use. In his hand he held a sixteen-inch wire hook. A few feet away lay two large white-feathered roosters' bodies, twitching and flinching reflexively.

The girls stopped abruptly and huddled together within good viewing distance of the action.

"What are you kids doing here?" interrogated their Father, "You should still be in bed!"

"But you said we could watch," reminded Windy.

Shanty added reassuringly, "We won't get scared."

"No way! We love this kind of stuff!" stuttered Bonky with anticipation and excitement in her voice.

"All right, but no noise from any of you Little Devils," (an endearing reference the daughters preferred to interpret to be synonymous with Little Divas). "And stay back!" demanded the Dark Warlord of Evil (an equally endearing title usually understood to mean Dear Dad of Envy).

The slightly intimidated Triumphant Triad nodded in unison as they complied with the fastidious rules and regulations befitting a coronation or a knighthood. The Little Divas obligingly satisfied their dear dad and quietly shuffled backwards, a bit farther from the theatrical stage.

The morning sun had still conveniently not risen, so in the half light of the morning dawn, the drama continued. With the wire hook in his left hand poised for battle, the Farmer stealthily moved toward a white sleeping rooster. He carefully hooked the rooster's ankles and with a quick jerk of the wire, he dislodged the hefty bird from its tree perch and rendered it upside down.

The comatose dinosaur derivative, spread its wings at a relaxed and noble distance appearing more like an eloquently festooned Drag Queen than a Ruler of the Roost. Without delay, the Farmer removed the axe from the surface of the stump and placed the bird's neck on the chopping block. With calculated precision, the Butcher cracked the air with a hard fall of the axe to the rooster's neck, severing the cocks combed head from its body. The bird's bloodstained intellectual center, dropped to the ground and rolled a short distance from the stump.

"See," said Bonky, "It rolled. It really did roll!" Windy and Shanty didn't bother to acknowledge their baby sister's potentially riotous observation.

The Axe-Man hurled the headless fowl off to the side. When it landed, it swiftly became airborne again. Its reflexive muscles powerfully tossed and turned the bird repeatedly as it ascended and descended in a ballet-like theatrical tragedy choreographed for a seasoned audience of macabre cynics and satirists.

The blood spray from the severed neck drew spirals and loops through the crisp October air. Finally, the decapitated winged entertainer settled in a heap near the first two headless carcasses, still twitching and flinching.

Bonky exclaimed, "Wow! What a sight!" She turned to look at Shanty and Windy and added, "Hey, I think we've been hit."

Windy and Shanty looked at Bonky and responded in unison, "Oh shit! How gross!" All three Farmer's daughters were dramatically spattered with fine droplets of fresh chicken blood.

Windy groaned, "I guess this means baths." Shanty and Bonky followed with extreme groans.

"Oh well," squealed Bonky, "it could be worth it. Five more beheadings to go!"

An audible, "ShShShSh!" from the girls' Father silenced them as he stalked another sleeping Master of the Dance. The sisters quietly spied an opportunity to examine the voice boxes inside the severed heads scattered on the ground. Before their Father returned to the chopping block with his next victim, the Three Illustrious Vixens scrounged sticks off the ground and poked the available throats within reach.

Squawking noises fired out of the disabled beaks like party horns at a birthday. The satisfied Vixens shrieked with delight then rearranged themselves seated on the ground with still a good view from the gallery, but a bit farther back than before. As they huddled together again to watch the next beheading, Shanty said, "I'm glad we don't live in the city."

"Yeah, me too," quipped Bonky.

"City kids are too naïve to appreciate this sort of excitement," insisted Windy.

"What's naïve?" inquired Bonky.

Shanty obliged with an answer, "It's just a nice word meaning stupid, stupid!"
"I'm not stupid!" Bonky retorted as she kicked and elbowed Shanty in the gallery seat next to her.

Windy scolded her two sisters and warned them, "Settle down or we'll be sent back to the house."

Shanty turned to Bonky with a firm instruction, "Yeah, don't wreck this day for us or we'll be doing dishes instead! This rooster stuff is good for us. It makes us smart. We don't want to be naïve like the city kids!"

Windy concluded with, "Yeah, we might become great poets, novelists or morticians some day. This training could be valuable. My teacher says that the great thinkers in the world are people very close to nature, people with courage and imagination.

"What's a mortician?" begged Bonky.

"It's someone who builds brick fireplaces, stupid!" clamored Shanty.

Windy laughed so hard, she lost count of the axe blows. She corrected Shanty and casually replied, "A mortician is a person who makes dead people look alive."

"Why would dead people want to look alive?" asked Shanty.

"How do I know?" said Windy, "The dead can't speak."

"Shit, I hope not!" droned Bonky.

As the decapitations and aerial dances continued, the Inspired Infidels also continued to argue and cross-examine each other as topics fermented. Following a short meditative evangelical pause, Bonky summarized her cataclysmic thoughts, "Do roosters go to animal Heaven?"

Shanty answered, "No. There is no animal Heaven."

"Why not?" countered Bonky.

"Animals have no souls," Shanty definitively remarked.

Windy straightened her back from a previous gladiator slouch and informed her sisters with guarded ostentatiousness, "People don't have souls either; and for your information, there is no Heaven for people either."

Shanty and Bonky also straightened their previously slouched gladiator backs. With index fingers wildly pointing directly at Windy they hissed, "Sinner! Sinner! You'll go to Hell for that!"

Windy calmly hissed back, "There is no Hell."

"How do you know?" demanded Shanty.

"Yeah, how do you know?" echoed Bonky.

With the uncanny presentation of a Professor with tenure, Windy paced her words, "I simply know that Heaven and Hell are imaginary places that naïve people create in their minds."

Shanty and Bonky glared at each other with dangerous skepticism in their unretractable voices as they simultaneously exclaimed, "Shit!" for lack of a more intelligent well thought out word suggesting Armageddon and it's deeply extolled beliefs.

Shanty was the first to challenge her older sister, "What about God? If there is no Heaven, then where does God hang out...besides EVERYWHERE?"

"Yeah?" agreed Bonky.

"There is no God," said Windy.

Shanty and Bonky irrevocably stated, "Shit!" with heightened concern regarding the implications of a lost concept, but little respect for the deification of Godlessness.

Shanty wondered, "How will we tell our parents?"

Windy apprehensively replied, "We don't have to. They already know."

Bonky pouted, "Then why do they pretend to believe in God and Heaven and Hell if they really don't?"

Shanty also pouted, "Yeah, why would they want to trick us like that?"

Windy resolutely sacrificed a gamble, "Do you like getting money from the Tooth Fairy and presents from Santa Clause?"

"Yes! Yes! We do!" sobbed the two girls in unison.

Their attention was suddenly diverted back to the stage of fowl carnage. The morning sun skirted the horizon and threw subtle beams of light that penetrated the Coliseum of Terror. With one final calculated precise stroke, the Butcher cracked the air with a hard fall of the axe to Number Ten, severing the last cocks-combed head from its body.

With similar gravity of thrust, Windy also dropped the axe, "Well," she uttered with deliberate hesitation, "the Tooth Fairy and Santa Claus do not exist, and nor does God; but most people like to think they do."

Bonky cried, "Shit! The Tooth Fairy?"

Shanty blurted, "... and Santa Clause?"

Together they cried, "They don't exist?"

"Of course not," reassured Windy.

A prolonged and saturated lamentation emerged from the vocal cords of the two devastated younger siblings. It was as if their voice boxes were being prodded with a stick.

Shanty finally acquiesced mournfully, "Oh well, at least I won't have to worry about going to Hell anymore."

Bonky agreeably gargled a moan, "Yeah, me either."

The slaughter was over, but not the punishment the two traumatized siblings cohesively decided their philosophically brilliant older sister deserved.

Before their Father disengaged from his chores, Shanty and Bonky repeatedly kicked and flogged Windy as she tumbled back and forth between them. The young Professor cradled her precious head in her skinny-jacketed arms and laughed unabashedly at her sisters' unsuccessful attempts to suppress her influence and individuality. The psychologically agonized pair of Monstrous Child Tyrants failed to harm her.

All three Divas quickly rose to their feet as they noticed their Father approaching the viewing gallery. With an unmistakable sigh of disgust and a tempestuous shake of his head, the Farmer looked upon his blood-spattered, grass-stained, dirt-encrusted, lack-luster daughters with recognizable disenchantment.

The pure, angelic, youthful darlings he might have hoped for, was a mere fantasy. Like a harbinger of predictability and rationale, he liberated them with an exhaustive but gentle command, "Jesus Christ! You had better get cleaned up or your Mother will disown you!"

The Three Little Maidens raced to the gigantic outdoor wooden rain-barrel full of cold water. They tore their clothes off as they scrambled head over heels to be the first immersed. The masochistic fiasco resulted in a rejuvenating sequence of primeval ceremonial cleansing. The Barbaric Babes ritualistically soaped and scrubbed themselves and lathered each other's bountiful discolored locks. Their wet bare skin shivered and their teeth chattered in an arpeggio of vocal sputterings.

Bonky in particular, entranced the chilly sun-drenched October morning with, "Jesus Christ! No Tooth Fairy... No Santa Clause... No God... No Tooth Fairy... No Santa Clause... No God... No Tooth Fairy... No Santa Clause... No God..."

Shanty jerkily pleaded and intercepted Bonky's repetitious soliloquy with, "I... hope... later... we... can... watch... the... feathering... and gutting... of... the... roosters!"

"I'll... make... sure... we... can," shivered Windy in a goose-bumpy staccato voice.

Poem #11
Homage To Winged Creatures

All Three Little Children
Gathering in the dawn,
Making feathered outfits...
Heavy when put on;
Waiting for the sunrise
To launch their suits in flight,

Without a rocket boosting them,
Their wings will have to
Fight for height,
As dreams propel them
Far beyond their native Earth
And out of sight.

Their eyes will scan the cosmic map
For figments in the sky,
With hopes of counting endless swarms
Of Fairies drifting by.
But as they search galactic space
With sunbeams at their sides,

No sacred God resides
Amid the stardust coliseum
Or the gemstones cast among them.
Venus bears no garland wreathes
And Mars no warring shields;
Mercury hides its silver side

In darkness, without pride.
Jupiter flaunts a fearsome mass,
But isn't unlike weather;
Spinning as a hurricane,
Its force... a natural tether,
Keeps no phantom unicorn

90

Connected to a diamond core
Dwelling at the planet's center.
Youngest in her feathered suit
Succumbs to Giant's pressure,
Tumbling downward swiftly
Through the Giant's rings of censure.

Two remaining Travelers
Wave adieu with wingtip flutters.
On to farther realms they soar
For astronomical adventures.
Ahead turns Saturn without ale
Or other jovial waters;

Uranus sleeps upon its side,
With rings about to scatter.
Neptune rests among its moons
Devoid of Herculean tide;
Pluto has no Underworld
Or River Styx to battle.

As Middle Child hurdles by
She's taken down asunder,
Not by Pluto's gravity,
But dreadful silent thunder.
It is a gap of awesome depth
And captivating wonder;

A prompt adieu to fallen plight
Of unrecovered Pilgrim,
As Oldest Child seizes hope
Avoiding blackest matter.
Event Horizon atomizes plunder,
Coercing solitary flight.

Remaining Child armed with Truth
And clear of opposition,
Suddenly spies a brilliant cloud
Of widespread congregation;
An entourage of white-robed forms
Emerge with bold ambition,

Mocking with a flash of grace
The Astronaut's awareness,
Of Kuiper's comet field of lace
Along the frozen edge of space,
A natural escapade of beauty
Far exceeding cannon duty.

A backward glance at Earth's domain
Reveals a sign of danger.
A glowing coalition's rage
Overwhelms the planet's reign;
With warfare's rampant fatal loss
A Red Dwarf raids the manger.

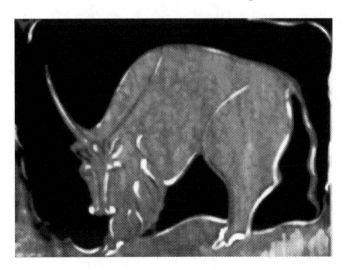

Recipe #16
Sweet And Savory Curried Lamb Wraps

-Pre-cook Basmati rice with curry, honey, garlic and mango chutney.
-Arrange rice on wrappers covered with Gouda cheese slices.
-Top the rice with strips of grilled lamb and cooked beets, raw zucchini, portabella mushrooms and apples.
-Roll up the wraps and bake them until hot and the cheese is melted.
-Serve with a mixture of sour cream, yogurt and lime juice.

Presentation:
-Serve this lunch on a Saturday.
-To complete, wrap up your imagination in erotic behavior to follow.
-Ideas could transpire on the table, cloaked in a checkered red and white cloth, with a vase of red and white carnations, carefully relocated to the floor.

Recipe #17
Sweet And Savory Duck Wraps

-In the center of a wrapper, layer slices of Edam cheese and cooked strips of marinated grilled duck.
-Drizzle spicy Thai and orange sauce over the contents.
-Add pre-steamed lengths of Chinese greens, pineapple and red peppers.
-Roll the wraps up snuggly.
-Bake until they are heated through and the cheese is melted.
-Top with a spicy sweetened clove and nutmeg apple yogurt sauce.

Presentation:
-These wraps make a fine Sunday brunch at your bedside table, richly adorned with blossoms of eggplant scattered over a purple tablecloth and your lover's sleepy, half-naked body.
-The remainder of the day should dictate it's own carnival of bedroom festivities fraught with unforgettable passionate mollycoddling until fatigued or revitalized.
-Avidly yield to whichever consequence prevails.

Chapter 8
Advancing To The Tube And Stuffing It

The Alaskan King Crab dinner party was positively the impetus required to re-ignite Helena's beguiling propensity for amorous cravings. Her salacious yearnings for victuals meticulously prepared, began to threaten the overwhelming writing schedule that she had so recently adopted.

She thought in all likelihood, advancing to a higher level of culinary creativity might punctuate and define her amorphous roles as yet undetermined by greater beings of outstanding intellect and skill.

Although Helena was feeling inadequate as a Goddess for temporarily misjudging her focus and direction, she still felt visionary. Her ascension toward honorable recognition among ethereal Culinary Judges provoked a renaissance of potentially controversial remedies for malnourishment.

Helena fathomed that nothing could be more primitively natural than a dainty reception of broiled fragments of human artifacts extraordinaire. Cannibalism within one's tribe, she surmised, was possibly a well accepted tradition practiced under a full moon in a jungle temple built of palm fronds, small offerings for sins committed. Self-torment might have exonerated and cleansed the guilty, like self-gratification might have rewarded the substantially generous.

Helena was certain that she had no cannibalistic tendencies whatsoever, but she fantasized otherwise about Clarise and her lesbian lover. If given the opportunity, Helena felt that Clarise would in all probability, pre-select the offerings of her previous male incompatibilities with utterly joyous scrutiny. Genital odds and ends, digits, and lobes would suffice on Clarise's kabob rack. Helena would simply have to invite Clarise and her partner for dinner and social chat.

They all would delectably slice their way through sausage-stuffed calamari tubes, pale anemic spears of asparagus, fleshy oyster mushrooms and juicy rotund figs, swollen from a creamy wine sauce smothering the orgy of mated candidates.

Like foreskin, the calamari snuggly encased the accurately hand formed penis-like inner protuberances; the large labial mushrooms loosely wrapped the penetrating blades of the white, blanched asparagus; and the gonadal ovarian-bloated fruit orchestrated a symphony of splendid genital-like offerings. Emblematic flesh and blood sufficed as penance or an act of contrition. Willfully spent gifts of self-inflicted torture might have been alleged to appease the Gods and Goddesses for the sins of loved ones that had passed away.

Shedding an antler, winter coat or reptilian skin; losing a masticating molar or dispensing of fecal debris or urinary detritus along a natural pathway between birth and death in the animal kingdom, could be the anthropological link to the spiritually credulous formation of stars, galaxies and the entire universe.

The richness of minds, ideas, inventions and creations born of civilizations; the instinctive desire to survive and conquer alchemized with the fear of death and destruction; the human condition aside, we worship oblique supernatural and unsubstantiated mythical fantasies, thought Helena.

In an attempt to design and structure the universe she concluded: like architects, we construct monuments from the fantastic splendor of our juvenile dreams; we erect disaster-defying shelters; and like children, we search for happiness, love and success. We search for wisdom, pleasure and laughter; we search for companionship; and ultimately we seek immortality. While desiring immortality, we become the Gods and Goddesses within our furtive means, which we are intended and entitled to become, while earnestly exploring the source of where we have come from.

Advancing to the tube and stuffing it was simply Helena's way of pursuing the lightness of being, in concurrence with the incredible weight of not being. Cannibalism would ensure devastation of the species. But in metaphorical jest, it could inspire communication within the species.

A knock at the door indicated the arrival of the librarian and her mate. Helena received a bouquet of flowers, an evening gift from Clarise. For Napoleon, she had a cool handshake. Clarise's friend Daphne, had a smile and a warm handshake for both of her evening hosts.

The heavenly scented meal was still in the oven, emitting a glorious aroma of nutmeg, cloves and orange zest, a trinity of savory garnishes selected by Helena, the heroic Goddess herself. She assumed her choice of symbolic delicacies would endure communal approval. Nonetheless, in Helena's flurry of assessment, the eventual presentation of little roasted shrunken penises, labial representations and sweet gonads, did not entice Helena's guests.

Clarise and Daphne abruptly revealed their strict vegetarianism, a detail not mentioned in advance. Should she have asked them earlier, she wondered? Helena remained calm and undaunted by her guests' refusal to partake of the allegorical mutilations. She relinquished her pride and telephone ordered a meatless pizza for the ill-witted ones, while she and Napoleon relished in the flavors of every suggestive humanoid morsel and tidbit available.

The hosting pair gracefully concluded the meal with a supremely robust, rosemary/vanilla/rum custard dessert topped with a painterly display of inverted fresh raspberries, resembling a rabble of succulent nipples.

The lesbian guests abstained from the herbivorous dessert as well as the carnivorous entrée, exposing their fragile inhibitions, sulkiness and seemingly incurable incapacity to freely exchange dialogue within a non-hostile atmosphere. The respectfully delivered alternative victuals had no obvious effect on their grimness. They departed without a twinkle of congeniality or spark of appreciation.

The evening ended with an imaginative and courageous Goddess feeling sufficiently glutted, but slightly forlorn and dejected.

Recipe #18
Midnight Magic Without Clouds

-Let the music begin with an accordion, bagpipes or whatever instrument can be coerced into performing.
-Prepare a campfire that slowly develops into a hot bed of coals under a dark, starry, suspenseful sky.
-Toss into a heated wok containing garlic, butter, olive oil, and white wine: crab legs, shrimp, lobster, mussels and clams, all in their shells.
-Cook quickly, tumbling the seafood constantly.
-Provide raw vegetables, dips, fresh breads and exotic beverages on the side.
-Float burning candles on the fishpond.

Presentation:
-Provide a telescope for close examination of the sky.
-Offer large cloth lap mats and luxuriously sized napkins for guests.
-Crack and de-shell the seafood as it is consumed.
-Dance between bursts of cosmic activity.
-Children are especially fond of such events.
-Party until the spirits are gone, the wok is empty, the meteor shower has ended, the guests are mesmerized, the candlelight has faded, the music is no longer present and the children are yawning extensively.

Variation:
-A Lunar eclipse requires Champagne and an abundance of oysters, scallops and squid.
-Increased music and dancing is essential.

Poem #12
Third Nightmare

Fingers barely touching clouds
Determine the flight of tiny feet

Barely touching pools
Of rainbow colored puddles,

Where naked babies
Learn to swim, internally.

Barelegged minds
Walking among snakes

Devouring the ages of venom,
Rise instinctively to angels or demons,

Then sink forever into pools
Of rainbow colored puddles,

Where naked babies
Learn to swim, internally.

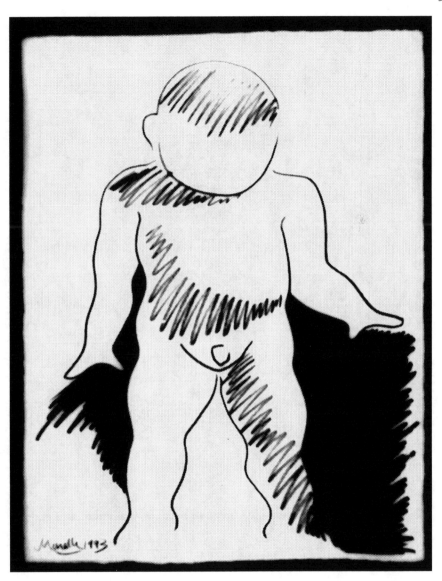

Excerpt From Helena's Book: The Three Sisters
Excerpt 3: The Maggie Episode

"I love springtime, because we can play outside!" said Bonky, as she and her sisters Shanty and Windy nested themselves and their dolls on a bed of hay beside the barn. An agreeable lunch of weekend macaroni, cheese, bacon and peas filled their insides.

A mob of cats tangled their tails around and about the girls' arms and legs and made them giggle.

"Yeah," said Shanty, "the dolls seem so much more alive in the sunshine. They are as warm as real babies!"

A herd of cows mooed in the distance as Windy lifted her shirt to expose her flat bare chest and exclaimed, "I'm going to have real live babies some day and I will feed them like this!" She demonstrated lactation by placing her diapered doll against her chest. The young biologically inept mother cuddled, rocked and hummed to the baby doll as she pretended to breast-feed it.

Bonky and Shanty laughed and squealed uncontrollably. They knocked over the empty doll carriage that waited nearby. Shanty said between bursts of giggles, "I will feed my babies with a bottle!"

Bonky replied, "I am not ever going to have babies!"

Windy added diligently, "Well, some people just shouldn't have kids at all. Did you know that a lady in this area baked her first newborn like a piglet in a roasting pan? When the dad came home from work, they ate it for supper, with peas, potatoes and applesauce!"

Shanty and Bonky gasped in revulsion at such a distressing thought, when suddenly without warning a truck approached. It grated and screeched to a halt next to the pasture.

Men's voices disturbed the spring air.

The girls dropped their dolls and rushed to the corner of the barn. They saw their Father talking to someone. It was the heavy-weight, fire-breathing Veterinarian. The girls knew at once that something might be wrong. They could see that one of the cows was lying down. "I wonder what's happened to Maggie," asked Shanty.

"She's probably sick," said Bonky.

"Or maybe she's going to have a calf," retorted Shanty.

"I think she's dead," whispered Windy.

As they all ran toward the pasture fence, Bonky and Shanty deliberately huffed and puffed. They were audibly procrastinating the piglet in the pan story. They both loved peas, potatoes and applesauce...but not anymore.

When they arrived at the fence, Windy asked, "Can we watch?"

The Vet grumbled, "Damn it! If you're quiet!"

As silently as she could, Windy reminded Bonky and Shanty, "Mr. Mashet is called to the farm only for very serious events, like the time when Heather the Holstein cow kept falling down. Remember?" she queried, "Whenever Heather tried to stand up, her huge black and white hide would tip over as if her legs were weak or her brain was dizzy!"

Momentarily, Windy demonstrated a noiseless but vibrant collapse. After a slight pause in a crumpled position on the ground, she scrambled to her feet and whispered, "The Vet had to exterminate her. And there were some chickens too," she added, "that stumbled around and around until they'd fall head over feet and couldn't get up again." The younger girls nodded as their memories gratified them.

Shanty mumbled out loud, "I wonder what they are going to do to Maggie?"

Bonky snapped, "Dam it! Be quiet!"

The Three Sisters watched in utter silence as the Vet examined the one half ton, motionless, ten year old milker. Mr. Mashet looked inside the creature's enormous slobbered up mouth. Then he lifted her tail for a close look at her shitted up rear end. Finally, Mr. Mashet pressed on the swollen bovine belly with repeated forceful nudges.

After some head scratching, nose blowing and tobacco chewing, the Vet privately consulted with the girls' Father. The two men nodded in agreement.

Mr. Mashet lumbered back to his truck and returned carrying a large bladed knife. He bent over Maggie's belly and with deliberate experienced strokes, he sliced it open. As Maggie's pressurized guts exploded outward onto the ground, Mr. Mashet abandoned the knife and plunged both of his rubber-gloved hands inside the menagerie of internal cud-choked digestive chambers.

Lacking all self-control, Bonky blurted out, "Jesus H. Christ, what the hell is he doing?"

In response, all three girls immediately held their noses shut in rapid anticipation of a deadly foul smell. Windy calmly replied in a rousing nasal voice, "Mr. Mashet is performing the autopsy to find out why Maggie died." After a lengthy gap Windy continued, "And I think he is holding the answer."

The Vet rose to his filthy boot-clad feet and approached the entranced trio of slightly horror stricken Little Maidens. He waved a wet, dark brown elongated object in the air and declared heaving and panting, "The old cow swallowed this here, big old, rusty nail." He bent forward to catch his breath, and then continued candidly, "It punctured her stomach."

Still holding her nose, Shanty responded, "That's gross!"

Bonky recapitulated, "Yeah, that's fucking gross!"

Windy threw Bonky a stern glare from above her shielded face, accompanied by a reprising kick.

Mr. Mashet raised his eyebrows and retreated to confer with the Farmer in charge.

Shanty warned Bonky, "If you get us into trouble, you're a dead duck!"

"Should we run?" squirmed Bonky, "Dad's coming!"

"Too late," groaned Windy as they all froze to the fence, still holding their noses, just in case.

"I think you kids have seen enough for one day. Now go and play with your dolls," ordered the girls' Father.

"Sure thing dad. We'd love to!" chirped Bonky.

The sisters freed their air passages and breathed unobstructed sighs of relief and reprieve for Maggie having died a natural death instead of expiring by conspiratorial implementation. Windy unhappily concluded, "Poor Maggie, she was one great bovine specimen, always exhibiting her finest achievement, perpetual rumination."

"Yeah," agreed Shanty, "she was one great cow, alright!" Like escaped convicts lunging toward freedom, the Victorious Furies leapt off the fence. As they skipped and cart wheeled back to their play area beside the barn, they could see Mr. Mashet tie a rope to Maggie's hind legs. With a pulley, the Vet hoisted the disemboweled carcass onto his truck and drove away.

The Farmer deserted his remaining herd of cattle and returned toward the house with the recent burden of events in every step. The somber congregation of remaining udder-bearing ruminants attempted to follow the Farmer, all in a row; but, the pasture fence confined their agitation.

Beside the barn on the warm bed of hay, the Three Graces quietly dismembered their dolls. Arms, legs and heads were haphazardly strewn all around. The over-turned doll carriage was filled with contentedly purring cats.

The Triumvirate of pre-pubescent siblings could hear the low vocal rumblings coming from the pasture as a gloomy shadow of their Father passed by. Windy sorted through the scatter of cast-off plastic appendages then reassembled her doll. "We'd better head back to the house," she suggested. "You two can paint a picture and I'll write a poem for our deceased Maggie."

"Sure thing," agreed Shanty and Bonky. Together, the Little Matriarchs tossed the remaining dismembered dolls into the carriage as the cats scampered back to their nests on the hay. Windy carried her intact pseudo-breast-companion in her arms.

The tired trio hummed inharmoniously as they arrived at the house in subdued form. The peaked threesome thumped their wheeled carriage of delicate cargo parts up the narrow staircase to their bedroom. A rattle, thump, rattle, thump, rattle, thump, bump, bump, bump, resounded through the small farmhouse. The clamorous echo the girls forged with charted ease indicated their expected return.

A carnivorous smell of supper emanated from the kitchen, and permeated the entire small dwelling. Somewhat lazily but methodically, the inspired Prima Donnas gathered together their art and writing tools and embarked on a memorial tribute to Maggie. A quiet and studious segment elapsed when Bonky announced, "I'm done!" followed by Shanty's utterance, "Ditto!"

Bonky and Shanty held up their picture for Windy to see. It was a depiction of Maggie's green grassy meadow, inundated with bright yellow dandelions. "Maggie loved eating dandelions," mused Bonky.

"Nice picture," said Windy.

"Now read us your poem!" begged Shanty.

"Yes," said Bonky. "We want to hear it!"

In delayed, humble, obligatory fashion, Windy stood majestically tall and upright. With great reverence and seriousness, she recited her poem:

"SURRENDER OF THE SPIKE:

Beneath the stars
Poor Maggie lies
In all her bovine
Splendor;

Her bloodshot eyes
And royal pies
Will always be
Remembered.

We loved her well
But not enough
To clear the yard of
Rubble;

And now we have her
Mighty ghost
To cause us mighty
Trouble."

"Oh shit! That's a complicated poem," claimed Bonky.

Windy groaned, "You're so naïve!"

Bonky emphatically demanded, "I am not! I am not!"

With predictable hostility, Bonky wildly kicked and shoved Windy. The flogged Poet finally put up her arms and yelled, "I surrender! I surrender!" But, Bonky kept attacking her oldest sister.

Windy laughed and defensively cradled her head in her arms and yelled for Shanty's help. But, Shanty didn't rescue the chastised Poet. In fact, she teamed up with her younger sister and helped Bonky attempt to immobilize the Superior One Amongst Them.

Windy roared and wailed with laughter as she tried to objectively psychoanalyze the primordial behavior of her siblings. Shanty and Bonky seemed further antagonized by Windy's disparaging lack of submission and defeat. Verbal surrender was not enough. Again, between gasping breaths and laughter, Windy registered a muffled, "I surrender!"

But the Evil Dwarves wanted Maid Marion to cringe with pain and cry real authentic tears. The wiry athletic eight year old struggled to remain unwavered by her sisters' staunch disregard for her welfare. The genetic collision at the intersection of her Terrorist Rivals seemed most extraneous and hideously complex.

Windy's endurance suddenly began to wane, when amid the rounds of pounding and kicking, she felt the decisive and unmistakable sensations of sharp edged teeth and fingernails. Between gasps of laughter and the realization that her younger Demonic Siblings might be incurably insane, the prize winning track and field star emitted from her powerfully trained lungs, a heraldic chant of seismographic proportions, " You Cannibals! Get the fuck off me!"

Not to anyone's surprise, their Father's voice shouted from below, "Settle down girls, or you'll be doing dishes next weekend!" The young Tribal Warriors instantly parted and fell absolutely silent except for the occasional grunts and whispered threats of future admonitions. Shanty and Bonky didn't need to be exercised in the meaning or implication of the word 'cannibal'.

They had been blemished with that accusation before, with an accompanying intellectual dissertation from the Siren. And now as before, they felt the same embarrassment and degradation, and the same determined desire to guillotine their Judas. More importantly, the three girls absolutely hated washing and drying dishes.

And, not one of the elementary inherent fruits of their Mother's womb wanted to be denied permission to attend the next weekend's event. The young bull calves were scheduled for castration. The tired and hungry damsels heard the call of their Mother's voice beckoning them from downstairs. It was time for supper.

Predictably, the meal began with prayer folded hands and an incoherent chorus of assorted octaves praising the Lord and thanking Him for the bountiful feast before them. No one thanked the children's Mother for cooking and preparing the meal and no one thanked the children's Father for hunting and foraging in advance. Each daily banquet was interspersed with the communal regurgitation of recent events according to whomever wished to reveal in truth or fictitiously elaborate for survival's sake, whatever might audibly embellish the occasion.

In reality, the girls' verbal contributions and giggles ultimately diverted attention from their unruly habit of redirecting certain cooked items from their plates to the floor underneath the table for Silky, the family dog, for whom they loved and trusted with every digestible secret they wished to share.

Food on the floor was considered inedible for humans, even though it underwent the usual pre-consumption blessing. But, it was an acceptable way to feed a family pet, especially when the contents of a particular boiled stew suspiciously revealed fingers and a floating male unmentionable. The sordid entrée followed the coincidental disappearance of a nuisance trespasser, old enough, and wicked enough to possibly bring harm to the family name and a cherished daughter's reputation.

The derisive and questionable presence of the sausage-like penile component and digital tokens of conjecture, did not escape Windy's observational scrutiny. The unappetizing vestiges were judiciously expelled from the pot that evening, one item at a time, to the underworld of the dog's domain.

Following supper, the studious academic Divas rushed with unfettered accuracy to their pre-ordained positions on the sofa. They watched their favorite, sanctioned, thirty-minute television show with meditative attentiveness, broken by excruciating fits of belly aching laughter. During commercials, the sisters bounced up and down on the sofa, straining and squeaking the internal springs until the intended piece of furniture no longer sounded or felt like a sofa. It seemed to have evolved into an undulating, lumpy, seasick form of wailing troll, slowly waking from a deep sleep under a bridge.

A fatigued, "Settle down girls," wafted from the kitchen, which clanged and rustled with the sounds of post-dinner exculpatory reorganization, cleansing and disinfecting. The kitchen was always a disaster zone and already well known to be made worse by the ornery, manipulative and collaborative attempts unfortunately pursued on a few desperate occasions, by the Dissident Daughters of Devilish Wit. They would rather flaunt their rising intellect by spending their evenings quietly challenging their unfinished schoolwork, than engage in battles over loaded kitchen sinks, a contaminated floor, a catastrophically scrap-encumbered dining table and a few abominably sticky chairs.

The Dissident Daughters' constant promises and oaths of repentance were merely feeble, disingenuous, tyrannical expressions of autonomy and leadership. These qualities were not understood or appreciated by the parents whose marital unions begot them as a result of love, circumstance, or error; they weren't quite sure of the reasons for their existence. All they knew affirmatively was that survival meant making decisions, seeking knowledge and sharing one's wealth and excess with no one except the family dog.

Poem #13
Fourth Nightmare

We need rain tomorrow.
We need rain to wash away

The blood on the grass.
His body, like a scanty

Pile of twigs raked together
Before the first snowfall,

Lies wounded and scarred.
His shattered spheres open

And his eyes fix on mine.
Immortality flickers,

And then subsides.
A flash of lightning

Erupts the night
And thunder follows.

Recipe #19
Introducing The Delicate Tongue
To The Delicate Tongue

-Oven-roast a whole beef tongue wrapped in bacon with onions, garlic, cloves, cinnamon sticks, bay leaves and sweet red sherry.
-Seduce tongue partially through cooking, surrounding it with a wealth of whole carrots, leeks, carefully placed beets, and yams.
-Drizzle the resultant juices over the tongue during cooking.
-When roasting is complete, chill the tongue and vegetables until the next day.
-Serve a portion of the chilled tongue, sliced for sandwiches with horseradish, mayonnaise and lettuce.
-Slice the remaining tongue and chilled vegetable companions, rendering them for a mystery soup.
-Create a broth from their juices, plus add additional liquids, flavorings and herbs to satisfy.

Presentation:
-Enchant your guests with a turquoise tablecloth boasting an ox-blood vase filled with wild yellow cowbells.
-Serve the soup and sandwiches to your most talkative visitors.
-Divulge the contents of the meal, only if your company inquires.
-With the same passion and desire they consume the tongue, prolong the mystery.
-They will surely resort to flattery before resuming conversations, in assiduous fashion.
-If the response is indeed positive or at least neutral and calmness prevails, consider applying a similar culinary treatment substituting tongue for liver, with soup and sandwiches also in mind.

Chapter 9
Defrocking The Artichoke...
Over and Over and Over

Helena felt herself to be truly a heterosexual human being. Her biological desire to be mated with a man and bear his children; her devotion to be matriarch heralding the sacred vows of marriage to undetermined distances; her desperation to guide her offspring toward monumental challenges; and her inclination to attain spiritual immortality in a sacred union of eternal marital ecstasy, were Helena's most critical ambitions.

Helena's wit and playfulness that she frequently displayed, camouflaged her only indomitable fear, that of kissing a dying lover or a child.

The true marriage of a man and woman, she believed, was the genetic union of the mated couple within their potential offspring. Napoleon and Helena would strive to discover the intricacies of themselves and the entirely new creatures capable of expressing their own unique humor, perspectives and interpretations of the universe.

Helena would want to emphatically know and understand the children she might one day give birth to. She would unequivocally attempt to love, cherish and respect the precious begotten sons or daughters that she and Napoleon could only randomly design.

While writing her book, Helena thought about impregnation. The maturing Diva inside her was compulsively flirting with the maternal matrix, constantly diverting her from her work. The incalculable destiny of a microscopic zygote wandering the starless inner vault of her womb was a concept that entranced her. As for conception, would it be immaculate or contrived? She answered herself with a swift inner reply. She would prefer the contrived, fraught with multiple orgasms, like the bulb of the steamed artichoke...leaf by leaf...layer by layer...petal by petal...dipped in lemon mayonnaise, slipped past the teeth, drawing more and more flesh toward the center...defrocking the artichoke...over and over and over...exposing the heart, then devouring it.

Another artichoke and another, consumed with embryonic intent, suggested a joyful and successful union of chromosomal magic. The procreative copulation proved to be enthralling. Napoleon had a natural passion for providing a copious sea of orgasms of escalating intensity until the final tidal wave of ecstasy released the pool of fecund sap deep into Helena's internal temple of fertility, the tabernacle wherein dwelled her precious egg. The heart of the intrauterine reproductive dance was waiting to begin.

Poem #14
Autumn Queen

Mother with her precious gold
Quivering in her feeble age,

Quietly waits on her Death bed
Dreaming dreams that make her cry,

Listening to the icy winds rush by.
At the top of a frozen hill

Frigid hands are rushing
Through her twisted hair.

She's old and yet more golden
Than a seasoned summer pear

Still Clinging to the bough,
Waiting for a final solar flare.

Hoar Frost mutely stalks,
Claiming Rose's round hips,

Raping with bitter force,
Ravaging and waging remorse;

Her furrowed belly must bear
The cold kiss of Despair.

Winter's militia appears
Like a dream; mysteriously,

White snowflakes reel around
Casting a net of iridescent Pearl

Illuminating tamaracks and dry grass,
Trembling in a whirl of leaflessness.

Lending emptiness to the scene,
Poplars bow and bare themselves

Not seeming to care whose
Faded clothes they wear.

Night falls and Nature's heart succumbs.
Her sequined clothes and jewels

Are crudely tumbled on her bed,
Like leaves scattered on the ground.

Death's White Knights settled on her
Like thieves not making a sound,

As they seized her final breath
And danced upon her barren mound.

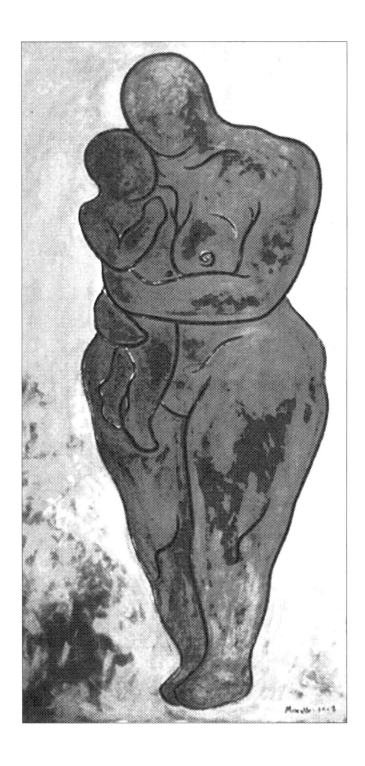

Recipe #20
Mussels, Noodles and the Garden Bounty

-Place in a skillet, chopped garlic, sliced mushrooms and large Kiwi mussels in their open half shells.
-Prepare a cream sauce with Mascarpone and Asiago cheeses, a licorice liqueur, white wine, whole fennel seed and saffron.
-Combine and simmer for ten minutes.
-Stir in precooked pasta, grated Parmesan cheese and pepper.
-Include a side dish of oven-grilled sliced zucchini, white onions, eggplant, sweet peppers and tomatoes.
-Season and toss with fresh chopped oregano.
-Serve with warm garlic bread and a pot of steaming Jasmine tea.

Presentation:
-Dine indoors during the first autumn frost.
-Request of your mate, wood for the fireplace and request of your children, service of the meal to a handspun, woven runner centered along the length of a wooden table upholding a large peach-bloom bowl of white baby's breath.
-The "Four Seasons" by Vivaldi, should accompany the dinner while collaborating upon past and present moral and ethical dilemmas.
-The young are restless and inquisitive, requiring love, guidance and reassurance.
-They will find these nurturing ingredients in most heartily cultivated meals and intellectually invigorating conversations.

Excerpt From Helena's Book: The Three Sisters
Excerpt 4: The Transformation

Between weekends, the Farmer's daughters behaved in their usual ways, exercising their tireless rivalries and competitive alliances in very sporting fashion.

Their differences were expressed like daily rituals at the Alter of Dissent. There was always a victorious one and a vanquished one or two at the end of every antagonistic encounter or militant disagreement. Rarely did the single-minded, controversial Princesses truly share a congenital truce by innate or tribal declaration. They each seemed inevitably destined for power, success or destruction.

Another highly anticipated episodic learning experience at the Sacrificial Alter in their Father's Ark of Animal Husbandry and Domestication, could only increase the distance between them and decrease their trust in one another. With limited advance knowledge of the ensuing event, all Three Innocents left their dolls tucked safely under the bed covers in their room for the duration of the afternoon at the barn.

The Vet would be there, helping the girls' Father acquire future behavior control by castrating the young bull calves. Castration resulted in a docile, non-reproductive, non-aggressive herd of steers favored for their lean cuisine.

The young female heifers would stand by, oblivious to the Torture Chamber that would claim it's male victims one after another, rendering them impotent and subordinate creatures. The heifers might eventually be artificially inseminated or pastured out with a full-grown prize bull for genetic prosperity and the initiation of a fresh herd of prospective milkers. Lactation would follow the resulting births of more offspring.

The continual cycle of agricultural regeneration became an established source of environmental influences that shaped and molded the conscious and sub-conscious dimensions of the Daughters of Wrath. Attending a castration was a new event for all three girls; however, Windy was responsibly armed with encyclopedic information and casual warnings for her two younger siblings prior to the unsanctimonious procedure.

Diminishing or postponing the girls' curiosity or desire for real live drama would have been impossible. They all thrived on the cerebral imprinting new experiences provided. Their thresholds for psychological stress, pain and terror impeccably challenged their infantile neural pathways at the indispensable acquisition of personal maturation and growth.

Feeling like a team of scientists and scholars embarking on a Darwinian quest for knowledge, the girls set off towards the barn, indulging in a synchronous marching stride. They didn't engage in any of their customary forms of conversation, ridicule or banter.

They strode in solitude, resembling a set of monks, sworn to a sacred oath of silence while seeking out the Holy Grail of Truth and Deliverance. With each step, they advanced closer to Wisdom. With each step, they molted their old skins. With each step, they aged and developed into their secret longings to be fulfilled as contributing members of society.

As the Reptilian Troop arrived at their destination, the Farmer and Vet had already separated the seven young bulls from the eight heifers and corralled them into a small pen. Unlike a slaughter, this afternoon's event was not likely to result in death. Despite the girls' awareness of that fact, their resolution to silence and their sustained grave demeanor was palpably detectable.

The Farmer and Vet took no particular notice of the omnipresent bystanders. The Two Despots resumed their scheduled business as each bull calf was systematically singled out, enslaved in a wooden device that trapped and immobilized the animal. This repetitive procedure reduced the task of castration to a minimum struggle.

The girls' Father was the apparent accomplice, raising the animal's hind legs to reveal the tender pink yearling testicles; while the Vet, owner of the large pair of pinching pliers commenced crushing the reproductive potential and gender characteristics from the bawling victim.

At the precise moment of ruthless demasculinization accompanied by an unrequiting bullish cry, Windy broke the silence and quietly remarked, "I'm glad I'm a girl."

"Yeah, me too!" replied Shanty and Bonky in unified relief.

As the second young bull was prepared for the shears, Bonky reminisced, "Until now, I always wanted to be a boy. I always wanted a penis and fuzzy little balls, but not anymore!"

"Yeah," agreed Shanty, "not anymore!"

When the Vet performed his task on the second bawling prisoner, the girls winced and snuggled their hands between their legs as if a primal instinctive force guided them to protect their own genitals as they sympathetically felt the crushing pain of the pliers. The agony of the young bulls felt like their own agony deep inside their cerebral vaults.

The three young Virginal Divas felt sick. One after another, they reflexively vomited on the ground. Unable to subject themselves to any further trauma, all three dizzy creatures held their abdomens and in a humble and highly discreet gesture of retreat, they slipped away from the Torture Chamber unnoticed, towards the house. The remaining bulls would have to suffer alone.

The disoriented fragile Princesses, felt a kinship closer than they had ever felt before. For the first time in their lives they longed to be friends and trusting mates for each other.

The recent skins they shed were layers of contempt and mischief. Their exfoliated debris was somewhere on the path between the house and the barn. Like brittle transparent snake skins, they left a trail of discarded fragments of themselves as they wizened and nurtured their unquenchable thirst for intellectual enlightenment.

The sisters staggered arm in arm, steadying and physically supporting each other in a collaborative attempt to ease the nausea and reach their destination as quickly as possible.

Their optimism diminished when Bonky vomited again, and stumbled to her knees. In a hopeless chain reaction of vomiting and stumbling, all three angelic forms lay helplessly sprawled on the ground with their phantom, bony, featherless wings outstretched as if in flight. They could have been mistaken for fallen believers in Icarus, drunken elves or seasick stowaways; but they were simply spent victims of their own curiosity and desire.

After a relaxed and motionless spell, Windy said, "I'd rather wash the dishes this afternoon."

Shanty replied, "I'll dry the dishes."

Bonky added, "I'll put away the silverware."

As the weaklings maintained their stationary positions on the ground, they could still hear the incessant wailings of the sacrificial yearling bull calves.

Exhausted and numb from the gravity of their predicament, the Trio of Tumbled Angels were unable to recover their strength and become the Domestic Debutantes they verbally committed themselves to, just moments earlier.

The only purposeful activity The Three Sisters appeared capable of accomplishing that afternoon, was induced by an unspoken collective involuntary decision to sleep. They didn't attempt to combat the seductive force or resist its nocturnal magnetism.

The afternoon guardian sun shone down upon them, warmly anointing the Vulnerable Vixens for their compassion and fortitude. They slept in anguish as hypnotic dreams flung them to and fro in the opalescent shell of a half moon. In designated time, they would become whatever manifestations they were destined to become.

A metamorphosis had begun. Presently, they were bound together by circumstance and the rotational laws of the planet they shared. But later, they might part with the severity of surgically separated conjoined triplets, hideously unified one moment, then optimistically individualized the next. Death to one, two or all three of them might tragically summarize the pursuit of genius and perfection, wisdom and success.

When the day's deeds ended, the Farmer came upon his bewitching daughters, still tranquilized by their unintended aversion to travesty. Having deciphered the telltale signs of their escapade, he shook his head in casual disbelief. With a custodial call for supper, the Farmer's parental disruption awoke the Sleeping Nymphs.

They groggily scrambled to their feet with the eagerness and haste of newborn gazelles indelibly inscribed to flee. And flee they did, to their castle in the attic.

The arduous rush up the stairs, two at a time, was hampered predictably by their impaired co-ordination and generalized weakness from sickness and lack of replenishment. Without a moment's hesitation, all three invalids fell into their common bed and escaped under the covers.

Their dolls were still there, where they left them, unfettered by the afternoon's crying of the bulls. In the darkness under the covers, the self appointed Surgeons delicately removed sticky taped paper penises from their make-believe babies.

The cosmetic male genitalia that frequently embellished the dolls' plastic bodies became an embarrassing wad of tissue paper stuffed under a pillow, to be reckoned with later.

The Infirmed Juveniles waited a short while for their Mother to arrive at their bedside.

She had an uncanny sense for recognizing trouble, so when she appeared like an apparition in the dusk, she asked, "Would you like some soup and bread?"

The girls hadn't prayed for this peaceful offering, but they desperately hoped someone would come to their aid and pamper them until morning, when they fully expected to feel normal again.

But the normal state of existence they had once been familiar with, would never be theirs again.

They would never again share a common desire to witness theatrical tragedies at the barn, their fantasized and highly regarded Great Theatre of Dionysus.

Moreover, they would never again want to be boys.

Accordingly, they would never again refuse to help their Mother with the dishes, or any other domestic chores when asked.

Their gainful knowledge would be attained through ingesting material from reference books in the library, academic textbooks at school and advancing media technologies.

Their journey into femininity would be characterized by harsh internal pain, secretly shared with the moon on sleepless nights. By Nature's inquisition, the morning sun would find them in bed crying, with their menstrual blood soaked sheets beneath them.

Eventually, the Pubescent Darlings would blossom. As enigmatic young women, they would flaunt their vibrant inclinations, discover their orgasmic entitlements and explore their potential genius with exhilarating effort.

Collectively, the girls would represent centuries of critical genetic mass. Individually, they would illuminate a faint glow from within their personal sacred interspatial galaxies to the degrees in which their diaphanous wings would permit.

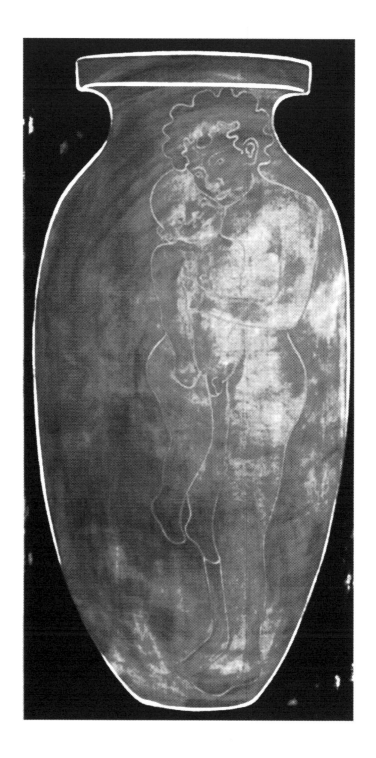

Poem #15
Requiem

Sleepy times, tear-filled rhymes,
Come sweet child,

Give us your eyes, your dreams
By the fireside.

We won't criticize or scold you;
We're too frightened to unfold you.

We need a place quieter than a pond,
A song lighter than the air at dawn.

Lying in your brother's arms conceals you;
Crying like a newborn babe reveals you.

Nothing left unsung has veiled regret;
Nothing left undone has mortal debt.

Trying to survive is Nature's hold;
Dying with a dream is Olympian gold.

Recipe #21
Trinity Spaghetti with Yard Long Green Beans

-Cook ground beef, pork and lamb in: tomato sauce, dry red wine, sweet sherry, soy sauce, Teriyaki sauce, balsamic vinegar, crushed chilies, curry paste, mango chutney, chopped garlic, and salsa.
-Add whole tomatoes, whole baby portabella mushrooms, small white onions, large zucchini wedges, chopped sage, and ground sage, basil and cilantro leaves.
-Simmer until the aromas impregnate the atmosphere.
-Serve hot on spaghetti with grated fresh Parmesan, Mozzarella and Gouda cheeses.
-Include a side dish of steamed yard long green beans with bright orange chrysanthemum blossoms.
-Prepare a warm pot of mint tea.

Presentation:
-Serve indoors during the first snowfall.
-Evade bad weather with a sustained fire in the hearth and any of Mozart's many musical tributes.
-Upon a snowflake-embroidered tablecloth, place a Chun-glazed pottery jug filled with a profusion of cool blue chicory.
-Engage your children in a deliriously rich discussion and analysis of sexuality and the cardinal virtues as practiced throughout history.

Chapter 10
Rooting Out The Almighty Truffle

Helena mused over her fanciful sketches, recipes, poems and disarranged excerpts of her book. She was looking for some order in the mayhem. Something was causing her to feel an uncomfortable chaotic doom within the helter-skelter assortment of signature accoutrements.

Helena's strange sense of foreboding seemed unusual and displaced considering she had just been informed by a physician, that the dance inside her had indeed begun and she was in fact not only pregnant, but was bearing twins.

By the time Helena returned to her abode, flushed with excitement and transitional bliss, a perplexing sense of calamity overwhelmed her. When the expectant female entered the apartment, she noticed the familiar scent of Napoleon's naked body, wet hair and coffee aroma on his breath from that morning when he kissed her and made love to her. But Napoleon wasn't there as he intended to be, in anticipation of a declaration worthy of a most significant intimate celebration. He left his classes early, a phone message revealed; but he did not arrive at their small palace in the sky.

A second message contained disastrous news. Helena's Napoleon lay frighteningly motionless in a hospital bed, dying from the impact of an over-zealous city bus rushing a red light at the intersection of the Law and Medical buildings.

When Helena entered the Emergency Room, a mangled bouquet of roses, thoughtfully retrieved by someone at the scene of the accident, now lay wilted on Napoleon's bedside table. The flowers had been intended for his incubating mate. Helena had never before felt such anguish and terror.

She and her Napoleon would not fall into each other's arms as planned. They would not share the intoxicating revelation of fetal clones, mirrors of each other's genetic cellular construction. They would not celebrate together, a gestation of double happiness.

The maternal Goddess and her mate would never share the joy of rooting out the almighty truffle between silk sheets, abandoning themselves to gentle squeals and grunts like piglets in a field investigating the truffle scent beneath the rich decay of earth, exploring candidly the ecstasy of making love with evolving babes between them. The lovers would never embark on another engagement of secrecy or laughter together.

The twins held in protective custody inside their mother's pelvic chamber were incapable of meeting their father or bidding him farewell. On behalf of his children, Helena commemoratively bestowed upon their beloved father's pale cheek, a final touch of her hand with a whispered promise of everlasting remembrance and a grievous admission of inestimable sorrow.

The devastated Goddess kissed her dying Napoleon, as his last breath faded from his fractured body. She folded Napoleon's lifeless arms around his burdened Goddess and two babies cradled within her powerful Oath of Motherhood. The care, sacrifice and guidance she solemnly pledged Napoleon's infants would immortalize her infinite love for her mate and signify her eternal affection for their young.

Napoleon's gold ring became Helena's, as her youthfulness irretrievably shattered. She was forced by Death's enormous gravitational influences to succumb to a harsh maturity, tragically and instantaneously. In a matter of months the Goddess would be holding and suckling at her breasts, two illuminating creatures of dependence and beauty, creatures of inertia and brilliance.

As Helena compiled the last few excerpts of her manuscript, her babies swirled and tumbled inside their amniotic universe as they neared the end of their internal existence. The pregnant Venus could still faintly detect the pallid scent of recent memories and quenchable desires within the vacancies of the apartment. The unforgettable attempts to conceive and visualize their future parental commitments and strategies together strengthened her private convictions.

She composed poems for her departed Napoleon with immeasurable sadness and longing for him; she faithfully wore Napoleon's gift of topaz, the orderly sequence of translucent blue gemstones around her neck, fingering them constantly; and she invariably continued to make chocolate soufflé. Helena ritualistically engaged her tongue along the inside of the bowl when she finished the dessert, just like Napoleon indulged in a similar courtship ceremony with her, sometime ago by the lake.

The abandoned and forsaken Goddess did not imagine securing a new mate, but she did hope to inspire a provocative dynasty of intelligent creative beings in search of joy, humor, and inventiveness. The inexplicable source of life and the elemental equation for death would be revealed eventually in stardust, born of traumatic cosmic collisions and reformations.

She approached a book publisher while she was still comfortably able to mobilize her extenuating physique.

All Helena could do now was mourn the absence of her culinary companion. She lovingly embraced the vase of Napoleon's ashes and kissed the two gold rings on her finger. The Voluptuous Venus nervously awaited the triumphal births, and looked forward to a new unfolding objective.

Radiant, with a warm amber glow and tears in her emerald eyes, Helena poached three simple eggs; one for the unhappy widowed Goddess and two for the playful, buoyant heirs still curled inside the fluid globe of her moon-shaped abdomen, now just a crescent away from being full.

Like an indeterminate scattered array of small pebbles, the Madonna's prenatal days were numbered. Helena wondered if her bountiful delivery could exceed all projections and ambitions intended for her modestly preordained literary future.

The solitary Goddess began to envision a workplace, with her children central to its function... large studios where color and form might reign in majestic severity. She could revolve around her children like a planet circling two suns... orbiting around binary stars in an elliptical path... clear in its tranquility... unknown in its destiny.

Helena swelled with purpose, as yet ambiguous, but fortified with inimitable cohesion and identifiable direction. The Goddess could feel the amplification of her gastronomic kingdom expanding out of the artistry of her primeval ancestors who carved small pregnant figurines, and erected temples toward the celestial firmament. She could hear the resonance of her kingdom's dimensions beginning to exceed its origins.

Helena could finally appreciate and somberly contemplate the full burden of the paired fruits of double happiness cocooned within her. As she slipped in and out of consciousness, moaning with the rhythms of her escalating respirations and pelvic discomfort, intensive visions of Helena's fearless Napoleon galloping high astride his gray Arabian steed, seductively enveloped her. The Equestrian Apparition dismounted and tenderly kissed the Goddess' engorged breasts and distended abdomen. Helena's yearning for Napoleon kept him near enough to disillusion and pleasantly comfort the anxiety of her primiparity with his soothing phantom presence.

In harmony with the returned immortalized spirit of Napoleon that mysteriously awaited the deliverance of his progeny, a swarm of matriarchs attended to Helena's earthly maternal needs.

A vital contraction signaled the gravid Venus as a swirl of amniotic fluid drenched the blanket beneath her. Birthing had begun. Under a canopy of evening twilight, Helena would soon be bearing down.

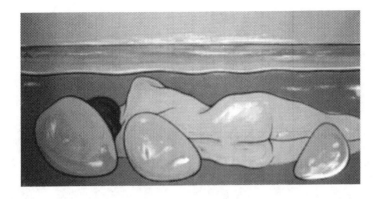

Poem #16
Collapse

Quiet and unmoving
She was on the floor;

As if she had fallen
In her sleep,
From a heavy dream
Or from weeping.

All of her lovely limbs
Fashioned in a long heap
Were folded,
Green upon green.

No shattered
Blossoms scattered
As petals, lay where
Her head rested;

Just lifelessness,
Where effort
should have been.

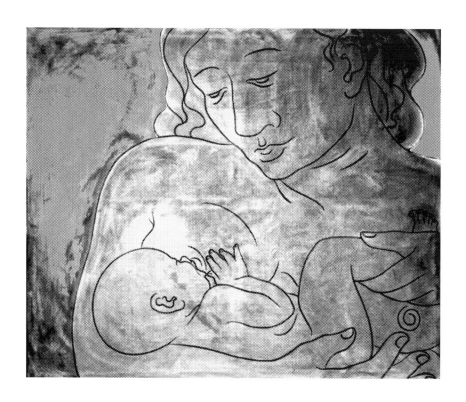

Recipe #22
Ecstasy For The Encumbered

-Prepare a simple, wholesome and tantalizing broth made from exquisite, favorite ingredients served with a light golden loaf of fresh bread.
-The entire postpartum feast should be plentiful in volume and bereft of potentially offensive spices, spirits, stimulants, roots, bulbs and herbs.
-Suckling newborns are wanton creatures of the universe, severely discontented if not satisfactorily idolized with the luxury of pure sweet maternal milk, unblemished by olfactory impurities and pungent flavors.

Presentation:
-Supply a bounty of garden flowers and gifts of natural sources with astronomical significance to enhance the meal and enrapture any Goddess delivered of her precious cargo.
-Provide softly burning candles to captivate and bind the eternally immortalized with the quantifiably corporeal.
-Newborn babes will cry for maternal and paternal protection and nurturing, despite one's substantive or ethereal uncertainty.

Excerpt From Helena's Book: The Three Sisters
Excerpt 5: Rocking The Cradle

When each of the girls reached legal age, in acts of defiance and autonomy, they changed their birth names. Windy became Wisteria, Shanty became Chantilly and Bonky became Belladonna.

Harboring the celestial qualities of an ethereal crystal ball, each of the Pilgrims wished for a glance into the future.

Wisteria longed to see the violent births and deaths of colossal star systems, and the beginning of the universe. She also hoped to gaze upon her archeologically exhumed ancestors throughout the world.

But, as Destiny courted Fate and Fate danced with Dreams and Dreams conspired with Reality, Wisteria died at the age of thirty, a novice but respected anthropologist and painter.

Although she celebrated her distinguished intellectual and artistic success and somewhat circumvented global adventures, she lamented her ensuing demise as she recognized and regretted the incurability of a progressive degenerative illness that compromised her daily pursuits.

Wisteria had maintained academic refuge in the city and bore no children. She sadly deserted her surviving lover with the promise of becoming iridescent stardust glowing eternally in the night sky.

Upon her death, Wisteria relinquished to her lover, a copper box of personal objects: swatches of colorful textiles; hand painted porcelain beads; miniature ceramic dolls and figurines; a collection of small pottery shards, broken seashells and faded photographs; love letters and vials of sand from a few foreign lands and exotic beaches.

Contrarily, Chantilly wanted to live in the country, raising a large brood of playful children, while serendipitously awaiting government assistance designed for the chronically unemployed.

But, as Destiny courted Fate and Fate danced with Dreams and Dreams conspired with Reality, Chantilly's few ideas and little ambition led to constant financial pleading from relatives.

She died penniless, at the age of thirty-seven while giving birth to her first offspring on a communal farm, after refusing medical intervention from a nearby birthing clinic. To quell the pain of a breech presentation, Chantilly desperately inhaled the essence of an hallucinogenic plant, nullifying the agonizing physical sensations during an adamantly prolonged and fruitless labor. A prematurely detached placenta, fetal distress and blood loss resulted in the mother's and child's eventual deaths.

Chantilly's surviving partners were frantically undecided whose stillborn child and wanton woman the dead were, when the medical officers, coroner and police arrived the next day.

Belladonna, the youngest of The Three Sisters, outlived everyone, except her own offspring. She fancifully desired to own and operate an exclusive gift shop representing artisans and craftsmen in her region.

But, as Destiny courted Fate and Fate danced with Dreams and Dreams conspired with Reality, Belladonna married a traveling salesman specializing in wholesaling Christian Bibles to schools, hospitals and hotels.

Forlorn and uninterested in higher education, Belladonna became a mother of five children with no opportunity to test her envisioned entrepreneurial abilities. By day, she became a profound kleptomaniac and in her limited spare time in the evenings, Belladonna attended activist meetings. She wasn't supporting animal rights or environmental safety; instead, she was a member of a subversive anti-abortionist group and a local chapter of white supremacists promoting racial hatred. Belladonna's parents also attended the meetings whenever they visited.

But, as Destiny courted Fate and Fate danced with Dreams and Dreams conspired with Reality, Belladonna's parents were killed in a car accident on their way home from a visitation and meetings with their daughter and grandchildren.

Years later, Belladonna's final waltz with Idleness, Intellectual Bankruptcy and Grief, found her suffering from clostridium botulinus, a toxin acquired by her own decision to consume unknowingly, the tainted contents of a home preserve. The resulting blurred vision, dizziness, slurred speech and difficulty swallowing, left her helpless and frightened.

Her children were all attending colleges and universities and her husband was away on business when Belladonna finally succumbed to the fatal consequences of botulism food poisoning. By the time an inquiring anarchist neighbor called an ambulance, she was unresponsive and consequently pronounced dead on arrival at the hospital. The cause of death was reportedly suffocation due to muscle paralysis.

Belladonna had reached the age of fifty-two without a glimpse of her daughters' destinies. Had she gazed into a crystal ball before ingesting her last supper, the embalmed Belladonna would have seen the youngest and most sympathetically dependant daughter, suicide following her maternal loss.

The remaining four impeccably healthy daughters became active secular humanists with doctorates in Archeology, Astronomy, Forensic Pathology and Bio-Genetics. Assisted by loans, scholarships and bursaries, they lectured and published papers evaluating deviancy, the penal system, atheism and cosmic entropy.

Their collective views were projected widely and objectively among scholars and laymen and women in every dynamic field of evolutionary and scientific study. As educated women of a beguiling nature, they challenged subversive ideology with courage and pride.

They were after all, descendants of an ancient matriarchal ancestry, steeped in vision, lore and Goddess worship. Like the diverse multitudes of ancient women born in the cradle of civilization and whose predated remains now occupied primitive burial sites and mausoleums, they too, were sisters of Venus and daughters of Lucy.

They were all children entombed in a complex interconnected solar system terminally encoded to scrutinize information, seek answers, question derision, and apply intelligent thought provoking solutions.

Unlike their mother, the deceased and buried Belladonna, each of the four aspiring daughters acquired extraordinary collections of beautiful and puzzling natural objects. They obtained intriguing artistic creations formed by human hands.

Each of the daughters discovered simple but evocative harmonies within the structures of the seashells, stones and bones they found. They marveled at the intricacies and emotional compositions of the sculptures, paintings, pottery and amulets they encountered and purchased with absolute reverence and admiration.

The collections the young women possessed, represented altarpieces of divine splendor, objects of which sustained their pursuit of the unconquerable.

As architectural monoliths, scientific discoveries and space travel symbolized human achievement, so too did their collections of valuable artifacts represent nature's resources and tools that contributed to human creativity and technological advancement.

Like precious pearls formed inside oyster shells on the ocean floor, so too were the daughters of the forgotten Belladonna, becoming beads for the universal necklace of human endeavor. Confidently, they embarked on a quest for infinite treasure, resilience and eternal beauty.

Chapter 11
Touching The Cord

Helena desperately struggled to appear comfortably in control of her alien circumstances, bearing down and pushing with every mitochondrial command available to her rapidly pulsating mother-ship of a pregnant body. Passivity, weariness and fatigue overcame the Goddess' conscious determination to expel her offspring. Repeatedly, each unrelenting powerful contraction brought her full-term inner inhabitants closer to their delayed but expected destination.

Helena's elusive spirit of Napoleon inescapably established himself between Helena's extended maternal thighs, awaiting the arrival of his twin babes.

Finally, with one last liberating push, fatherless and silent, the pair slid forth in a stream of blood and meconium-infused amniotic fluid.

Napoleon's disembodied apparition flowed over Helena's wilted body, covering her with a blanket of compassion and despair. Exhaustion left Napoleon's postpartum Diva shivering, but not breathless. A grim whisper entered her ear.

She responded with a groping terror and leaned forward. Helena touched one of the two umbilical cords and cautiously fingered the adjoining fetal remnants. At the place where life should have been, there was none.

Conjoined at their heads, the twins sprawled haphazardly between their mother's splayed legs like relics of an ancient civilization, archeologically unearthed for examination and display. Like ceramic dolls fused together by a demonic fandango of flames, the impish creatures of gothic resemblance betrayed their angelic facial features. Asleep forever, the tiny boys would never gasp for air, cry for food or whimper for affection. Theirs was a callous deathbed, not a cradle. Theirs was a burial ground, not a playground.

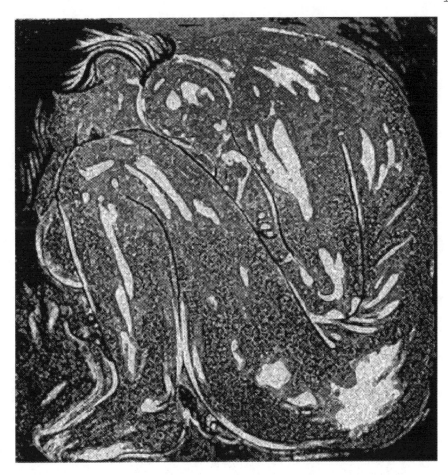

The anticipated magic of birth became an unpredicted assembly of death. Helena slumped back onto her pillow. She had been completely unprepared for such an outcome of her labor and months of optimism. The Goddess knew that she would have to devise a new plan, find a suitable resting place for her twins among the stars, and in the arms of their father's immortalized character. She would ceremonially unite the deceased trio by their ashes, the only remains of the dead. But first, she would weep, then sleep until dawn.

The End

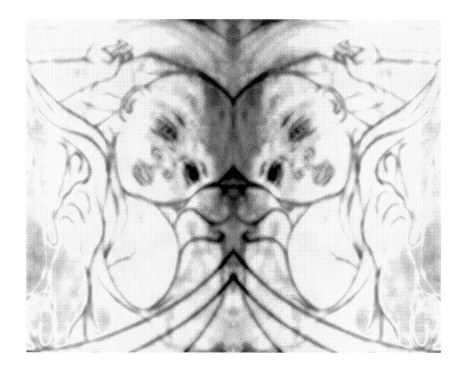

Poem #17
Prologue

Follow grand ideas until stranded,
Conquer every threat until abandoned.

Search the darkest space until surrendered,
Conceive of far off worlds while apprehended.

When you cease to further qualify or measure
Distant constellations' outlying cosmic weather,

Gaze with willful joy and fascination
Upon outcast planetary procreation.

Poem #18
Epilogue

When you stare into
Your willow pond at night

And see minnows quivering,
Lilies floating,

And dragonflies hovering;
When you find nothing missing,

Not even the subtle reflections
Of the stars above;

Then it's time to take a walk.
Begin a pilgrimage

Of undetermined destiny
And empirical design.

Conclude your journey only
When it guides you

To its rightful end,
And not a light year sooner.

By then, you will have
Laughed indelibly,

Cried uncontrollably,
And loved irrevocably.

By then, you will have
Forged paths through jungles,

Constructed bridges
Across crevices,

And lost a precious friend
To eternity.

If you return to
Your willow pond

And find it holds
A new star above,

You'll know it's time
To take another walk.

Begin a second pilgrimage
Of determined destiny

And unempirical design.
Conclude your journey only

When it reveals a feather
And a pearl.

By then, you will have grown wings
And become treasure.

Recipe #23
Wrapped Baby Beet Rolls

-Rinse and dry fresh beet leaves.

-Snip thin 2″ lengths of soft partially risen bread dough.

-Wrap each strip of dough loosely in a small beet leaf.

-Place each roll next to each other in an oiled roasting pan.

-Cover and place in a sunny location until the beet rolls are snuggled close together with risen dough visibly protruding from the ends of the rolls.

-Brush the rolls lightly with oil, then bake at 325 degrees for 30 minutes, or until the ends of dough are golden.

-While the rolls are baking, prepare a cream sauce with fresh chopped dill and green onions.

-Simmer until the sauce is slightly thickened.

-Add salt and butter.

-Remove the roasting pan from the oven.

-If the little heads of dough have stuck together during baking, gently separate and loosen the rolls from each other.

-Pour the steaming hot cream sauce over the tumbled, slightly cooled beet rolls.

-Serve immediately with grilled rainbow trout and steamed green peas on clear glass plates.

Presentation:

-Consider this a meal to linger over and share with children while manufacturing plans and building dreams together.

-Embellish the meal with intense humor and frivolous resolutions.

-Tremendous laughter will ensue.

-A white linen tablecloth with a hundred golden daffodils in clear glass vases will foster hope and congeal relationships.

Printed in the United States
By Bookmasters